GUARDIAN ANGELS BATTLE FOR HUMAN SOULS

GUARDIAN ANGELS BATTLE FOR HUMAN SOULS

DL RENDER

XULON PRESS

Xulon Press
2301 Lucien Way #415
Maitland, FL 32751
407.339.4217
www.xulonpress.com

Note from author:
Any references to historical events, real people, or real places are used fictitiously. Names, characters, and places are products of the author's imagination.

Paperback ISBN-13: 978-1-66286-160-4
Ebook ISBN-13: 978-1-66286-161-1

To my children – Stephanie, Erica, Michael, Amber, Alexis –
my days are rich with your love and respect.

Love God, chase your dreams and experience the experience,
where ever it takes you!

Prologue

Dear Reader;

My name is Birathos, and I am the leading guardian angel assigned by God to train, support, and guide newly assigned guarding angels. The angels' primary purpose is to protect and guide their assigned humans. I commission angels at the time of human conception. Our primary purpose is to thwart Satan's demons' efforts to corrupt human souls. Know that failure to keep the soul from doing evil and not repenting causes great anguish to the Father. Failure by a soul to repent may, upon its death, result in it being consumed at the demons' feast. We have assigned guarding angels to humans since the beginning of time. Christianity, Judaism, Hinduism, Buddhism, and Islam speak of guarding angels in their teachings. Their beliefs may dictate various protection tasks, but all have guarding angels protecting their charges. I have shared with you my letters sent to one particular guarding angel (Leuviah). As you are reading, note the trials and challenges this young man moves through in his life and the outstanding efforts Leuviah implements to keep her charge safe and in God's grace. In that the Father has given free will to his children, guarding angels cannot directly intervene in their charges' decision process. They may whisper positive influences but cannot directly cause the events to occur. We have trained the angels to protect their charges when danger occurs. One exception is if the human's name is written in the Book of Life. The Book reflects a specific date and time that the life is to end. As you read the letters and discover the wonderful work Leuviah has done to protect her assignment, it may cause you to pause and reflect on dangerous events in your own life that may have left you wondering how you survived. Maybe a medical professional told you it was a MIRACLE you survived, and you were uninjured. There are events in the proceeding letters that depict just that, instances when Leuviah wrapped her wings around Lyle (her charge), saving him from harm. The primary question is, how will Lyle grow—in Christ's grace or devolve to the lowest levels of corruption and evil?

Angel of God, Briathos

The Beginning

My prodigy Leuviah,

As lead angel responsible for guiding guardian angels and protecting God's children, I send this to you as our initial letter of engagement. Congratulations on your ascension to guardian angel. It is an exceptional responsibility you have embarked upon and must maintain diligence to protect Lyle from birth through death when you will turn over the soul to Azrael for ascendance and judgment by the Father. If the Father finds Lyle needs to atone for some sins through penitence, you will be responsible for escorting and guiding him through purgatory. In that the charge has recently come into the world, you have a few years to prepare for the protection and guidance to ensure success. Watch as the demons will be around the charge, his parents, and brothers/sisters. This will enable you to observe and learn their (demons') tricks that coax God's children to stray from His grace. This will add to your toolbox as you prepare to protect Lyle. At this time, Lyle will begin to develop, and his awareness of who he is as a person will become more apparent. Charges are flawed beings and are susceptible to negative influences by the enemy. Karael and Rizoel are good resources for you when urgent questions arise. I have assigned them to the parents of Lyle. They (Karael and Rizoel) have much experience in protecting and guiding the children to God. Demons are tricky and MUST be watched at all times, for they will trick the charge into falling from God's grace. There are some falls a soul cannot recover from and will descend to hell.

Lastly, you are responsible for the physical well-being of the charge (Lyle). This will be more apparent as he moves through his teen years and is driven by the enemy and friends to engage in risky actions. More to follow on this later.

In closing, remember love, compassion, and the love of God must be the mainstay in Lyle's daily life.

In God's grace, we thrive,
Briathos

My dear Leuviah,

I have reviewed all reports received by Archangel Michael. I commend you with pleasure on your efforts to care for Lyle as you have this first decade. The enemy tried to get him to steal candies from the local store. You whispered words of foreboding and guilt in his mind to dissuade him from committing the theft. This caused him to feel guilt and shame, resulting in choosing not to steal. You whispered, "Jesus would not like you to take that which is not yours." His parents have instilled in him a good foundation in prayer and attending services and remind him each day the joy in having a relationship with God. Because of your efforts, I am overwhelmed with joy, seeing the anguish on the enemy's foul visage each time you deterred their effort to move Lyle away from the Father. You will have to save him from serious harm in the future. On those occasions, you will know that his name is not on the list of souls to be taken to heaven yet. My friend, be ever so diligent in the coming years. I have reports that the demons have been successful in poisoning those around Lyle. This may eventually place doubt, anger, and abandonment in his relationship with the Father. A storm is coming, and you MUST be prepared to thwart the evil. Monitor the signs. The enemy on earth has strength and numbers. As you know, the goal of the enemy is to collect as many souls for their master before the end of days. Each lost soul will be at the evil feast, and they will devour the souls in hell.

Your brother in Christ,
Briathos

My sister in Christ,

Two years have passed since your last communications. Now do you realize the challenges that will be upon you in the turbulent age of the majority of years? The enemy will challenge Lyle as he has always done, quiet whispers, guilt, and new methods, "friends." Peer pressure is an overriding influence for young charges. Before we discuss the storm on the horizon, I mentioned in my last letter that I would like to discuss your efforts to guide the boy on the path of righteousness. Let us look at his consistent attendance at catechism and church services. He appears to feel the love and cheer of our Father. I have noticed you engulfing him with your wings, providing the additional warmth of love. On one occasion, the local seminary group was presenting their pitch to invite students to join the seminary. Something amazing happened. Lyle told his fellow students he wanted to talk with the seminary leader to discuss his desire to attend and become a soldier for God. This is the first step to becoming a priest and teaching the word of God. I felt the joy you and the other guardian angels in the chapel emanated on that day. The angelic light exploded and was felt in the heavens. Nice work. You see, his father was attending the seminary as a young man with the express desire of becoming a priest. At some point, the father met his mother and began dating. We suspect the demons were distracting him from God's training with enticements of the flesh. The father's guarding angel Rizole did all he could to keep him on track to priesthood. As you will learn, men are weak, and desire sometimes wins. God gave his creations free will; it is both wonderful and dangerous. Alas, as

Lyle is at the beginning of his teenage years, he would be influenced by those around him looking for excitement and danger. These influences eventually contributed to Lyle's decision not to attend the seminary. Again, free will is a tricky thing. Be not discouraged, for you are diligently guiding him. You will have challenges that must be overcome. I wish to remind you of another of your successes—while attending catechism, the building had a gas leak that endangered the students. Students and teachers were running around with adults yelling to get out of the building! Lyle was on the third floor, and you whispered to him that he needed to run out of the building quickly. Some students and teachers were passing out. He observed one student fall down the stairs. He ran out of the building. It surprised you when he ran out of the building past the police and adults. He ran all the way home, about one-half of a mile. We were laughing at your surprise and the silliness of humans under duress. Most importantly is that you did your duty to protect him by whispering to him to quickly get out of the building. Evil is coming for Lyle; watch Karael and Rizoel as they work with his mother and father. Reports from the guardian angel's office are that the enemy has infiltrated the emotional mindset of his mother, causing doubt in God, and being driven to lust another man. The mother has requested the father to move from the house and for divorce proceedings begin. Can you not see the anger in your young charge? He has no adult supervision, his mother is dating, and no longer wishes to care for her children. As you are aware, he is leaving his house and not returning for days and weeks. Evil is driving him to go wild with no regard for himself or those around him. As a fourteen-year-old young person, he should have guidance. I see you are attempting to do this with much effort and minimal success. Keep up the good work to protect him from evil. This is only the beginning of the storm. I see much danger ahead.

Keep shining your light,
Briathos

Leuviah, guardian of a soul,

Karael has reported the mother has slid further down to the enemy's side. She is entertaining strange men in the household while Lyle is present, causing him great consternation. Rizoel is concerned with the father's behavior. He has become distraught because of the separation from his children. He has been absent from visits with the children. Historical medical data shows the father had a mental breakdown a number of years ago. This was attributed to the mother's infidelity and pregnancies that occurred years earlier. The last two children were fathered by Lyle's uncle. He has become a lost soul. The demons appear in pairs at the father's side, whispering, "You are no good, worthless," "What kind of man allows his brother to father two children with his wife?" and "End your life." This is driving him into greater despair. Rizoel is patiently working with the father to return to God and receive peace from the Father's grace. I know Lyle's anger and depression saddens you. Know that you have done wonderful things to keep him from falling further into the enemy's clutches. This is a dangerous time for Lyle, considering the emotional events in his life and being just fourteen years old. He is young and malleable to demons' guidance. For a young man with no adult guidance, life can end in disaster if we are not at our best. You may not feel successful, but let us consider the events he has been involved in these past three months and your efforts to guide and protect him. The truck surfing incident—his friends badgered him, and, of course, the demons present, to stand on the cab of a pickup truck while traveling at high speeds. The driver touched the brakes, causing Lyle to fall forward from the moving truck.

You bundled him in your wings as he rolled off of the truck and to the ground. Your efforts protected him from the harm of the fall. You saved him from the oncoming truck that stopped inches from him. Except for a few scrapes and pebbles in his back, he was unharmed. He jumped back in the truck, and they headed home.

The shooting incident—Lyle has a "free spirit," enabling him to engage people from anywhere. He began associating with a group his town friends did not get along with. Many were of Middle Eastern culture, others were Vietnam veterans, haggard drug addicts, and kids not from his town. Locals were very protective of their home turf. Put testosterone-elevated young men in one area from differing backgrounds, coupled with the locals feeling their turf was being encroached on, and it can only end in conflict. His new friends assaulted some of his town friends. The kids he grew up with designated him an outcast. One night while hanging at the camp with his girlfriend, the town friends saw Lyle and were determined to beat him for his disloyalty. He saw them, jumped up, and ran along the river bank. Although it was pitch black out and no moon, he raced as fast as possible to get away. Suddenly, gunfire erupted from behind. He could feel his heart beating out of his chest. He was not wearing shoes. The ground with pebbles and stones were tearing into his feet. He was becoming short of breath, trying to keep ahead of the pursuit and praying bullets would not strike him! He came to a dam, the gate to the walkway, and his escape was locked. With panic in his eyes, he surveyed his escape options, the lake was in front of him, the dam to his right, and the pursuit behind him. For one moment, he thought, "They will shoot and kill me, alone and in the dark." Having no other options, he jumped into the water near the falls. It was so dark, and his only thought was, "If I jump into the water, they will not see me." Lyle ran to the edge of the embankment and leapt into the dark swirling water. You could see the demons dancing, encouraging the others to kill. The pursuers were yelling at him, "We will kill you, traitor!" They ran to the embankment searching for Lyle and began firing randomly in the dark into the water, hoping to hit him. Lyle was hiding under the bridge, fearing there was no escape. He pleaded with God to save him from this mess. You whispered, "Slide down the dam. I will guide you through the ice breakers." He swam toward the crashing waters, gauging where the drop would begin. As he hit the drop, he racked his brain, trying to remember where the ice-breakers were. The sound of the crashing water was so loud that he could not hear the attackers nor any other sounds. As he moved through the breakers, he thought, "If the breakers do not kill me, I will probably drown." The falls were pressing on him from all sides, and he was struggling to stay upright on his stomach. Leuviah, with your help, he maneuvered through the gantlet of the cement breakers. Considering the blackness of the night, the speed of the falling water, and his inability to see the breakers, he would surely have perished. You engulfed him in your holy wings, moving him through the breakers and to safety. Arriving at the bottom, Lyle floated safely down the river, swam to the bank, and walked home. During his run and escape through the dam, he felt his time on earth was numbered. He resolved that sooner or later, these guys would track him down and finish what they started that night. Leuviah, while reading your entire report, I realized this event was only the beginning of his problems. How you will keep him safe and on a path to God will be a challenge.

The beating—While leaving the park at night, Lyle was hitchhiking home, as always. While standing with his thumb out as cars went by, Lyle heard voices coming from the hill to his left, moving toward him, shouting they were going to beat him for his disloyalty. He was on a two-lane road with darkness all around, and he realized there was nowhere to run for safety. He had enough of being afraid of these guys and decided to take a stand against this evil. Beating or no beating, someone was going down with him. As the four men advanced, he stood his ground. The demons enraged, jumping up and down, pushed the attackers to "BEAT HIM." You saw the demons smiling with excitement, hoping the kids would kill Lyle, thus cementing those kids' souls to hell when it was their time to die. I know you prayed for help from angels nearby. Your prayers were answered. Suddenly, a vehicle came speeding out of nowhere, stopped, and yelled at Lyle to "GET IN THE CAR." Being angry at the attackers and tired of their threat, he defiantly yelled, "If you will fight me one at a time, I will accommodate you whenever it suits you." He laughed, and jumped into the car. The vehicle sped off, saving him a serous beating. I can only imagine your relief when Lyle was saved.

Leuviah, your charge is reckless; it will be a miracle if he survives to live past his twenty-first birthday. Not to say there is anything in the Book of Life reflecting this, but it will be touch and go. As you know, even when a name is in the Book for future accession to heaven, demons can disrupt this, causing a death sooner than written. That is why guardian angels are assigned to these humans.

The hitchhiking incident—The Demons were ever so busy attempting to corrupt Lyle. In this case, they enticed him, at fourteen years old, to hitchhike fifty miles from home with a friend to visit some girls. Remember, this friend is addicted to heroin and other drugs. I know Lyle is no "angel" right now. You knew he was experimenting with drugs. They visited the girls and were hanging with them behind the parents' house in a camper. The goal was for Lyle and his friend to sleep with the girls. Late that night, the father surprised them by entering the camper, assessed the situation, grabbed Lyle by the neck, and physically threw him out of the camper. You encouraged him to run before the father grabbed him again to beat him senselessly. That night the boys stayed in a dirty, cold, stinking public bathroom. When the boys woke cold and uncomfortable in the bathroom, they decided it was time to go home. But before heading out, his friend suggested they take some hallucinogenic drugs. It did not take long before Lyle could not see correctly, with "hallucinogenic trails" and images causing a misjudgment of time and space. Standing next to the highway preparing to cross, his friend darted into traffic, yelling, "Come on, let's go." The demons knew Lyle's judgment was impaired and were hoping he would jump into traffic and get hit by a car and killed. One particular demon was laughing and encouraged him to "RUN NOW!" It was jumping with glee. Lyle's heart was racing, scared, not knowing what to do, run or stay. He could not see properly. You whispered to Lyle, "Stay here and wait. All will be well." The demons took advantage of his fear, pushing him to run. Lyle looked to his left and could not determine where the cars were or how fast they were moving. Suddenly, he jumped onto the road and blindly ran. In your usual angelic effort, with automobile horns honking and cars swerving, you ushered him to safety on the other side. Wow! It enraged the demons for their failure to hurt him. You held him, providing calm as he "flipped out" after realizing the danger he had avoided. Demons screamed in his ear, "You should have died!" Lyle was sitting on the ground, crying uncontrollably, mumbling, "I should be dead." Your sweet, pleasant voice eased his drug-addled anxiety. After an hour, Lyle's friend patted him on the back, telling him, "Let's go home. It has been a scary day." When all was calm, they left for home. How is it that they were picked up by God's children? Hippies who love

God and drive around preaching the Word picked them up. They discussed Jesus and God with him during the travel. This provided additional tranquility for Lyle and some respite for you. The Christian hippies went out of their way and drove Lyle home. It is amazing how God's love can intervene when trouble is abound.

The drug-induced visions—Weeks later, I observed Lyle with his friends in a park. His closest friend, who was with him when he was almost killed in traffic, when he was high, pressured him to ingest LSD and snort cocaine. That evening while hitchhiking home on a dark and desolate road, he was so high that he saw nothing but melting colors, no roads, no trees, and he could not make out any shapes. Lyle stumbled into the road and back to the side, unable to get his bearings, and unable to figure out where he was. On the dark backroads, it is difficult for oncoming traffic to see what is in front of them. Leuviah, I know you were certain Lyle was going to be struck and killed. You guided him to a sign on the side of the road, where he sat holding on, unable to do or say anything. You provided calm and love during another difficult time, saying, "God is with you, Lyle. Stay and wait for help. All will be well." The demons were coaxing him to get up, hoping he would wander into the road and get struck by a vehicle. By the grace of God, his friends found him and ushered him to safety. The upside, because of your continuous care and guidance, after that miserable night, Lyle determined to refrain from continued drug use. I see the divine light that burns within Lyle. It needs continuous stoking with God's grace. During all of this turmoil, I observed, he, on his own, continues to attend Mass and confession. I see the love and joy he receives during and after services. This is the bridge to foster, even during hard times. Be faithful. Be courageous. The Father's grace is enough. God pours forth his abundant grace in every step of the way to bring goodness to them who love him.

God be with you in your efforts,
Briathos

My dearest Leuviah,

Based on your last letter, Lyle continues to be inundated by life's troubles. The previous events encompass the first few weeks of summer. Am I to understand he is still leaving home and remaining on the streets for one to two weeks at a time? Keep pushing him to go home. After all, he is only fourteen years old. I was sad to learn that after his last two-week sojourn, he arrived home to learn his family had moved out of the family home. It is understandable to see him angry and scared. The surprise and shock of discovering he no longer had a home must have been enormous! The demons were working on him to hate and be angry. They were laughing with glee to see the grief and sadness in this young man's face, saying, "You are so worthless. Your family left you without telling you where they went. Where is your God now?" It is my understanding that the his mother sold the home. Because of some legal issues, the new owner forced the family out earlier than the date agreed upon. Lyle thought, "I have nowhere to go." With your stoic and loving efforts, you reminded him that his grandfather lived next door. Lyle knocked on his grandfather's door. The grandfather answered the door. With tears running down his face, Lyle asked, "Where did everyone go? They left me." He learned the family had moved to another city, and he was going to live with his aunt and uncle nearby. I have seen the sadness he carries and how the demons work on him, attempting to boil the sadness into anger and hatred of everything in his life. Be ever so diligent, as I see the danger within him. I know his aunt and uncle have little influence in guiding him to a good and moral code. He arrived at his aunt and uncle's home. They told him his mother and siblings moved to another city. Lyle was to live with them. Weeks went by before another incident. He went to the camp and had been with a young girl. She had left "suck" marks on his neck. During their time together, she said to him, "I really like you. You would look really cool with a pierced ear. I have an earring you can put in it." Leuviah, consider what you may have done differently to discourage Lyle from these actions. When he returned to his aunt's place, they informed him his mother called, saying she was coming to see him that day. As I understand your description of the incident, here was Lyle dirty: no shoes, no shirt, marks on his neck, and an earring hanging from his left ear. His grandmother told him, "You better clean up and remove the earring before your mother gets here." His mother arrived, and after entering the house, noticed her son in such a mess and saw the earring hanging there. She angrily lunged toward him and pulled the earring out of his ear. His mother yelled at him, "You are coming to live with us. Get your things." While holding his bloody ear, he noticed a man with his mother. This is the first time he met his new stepfather. His love and respect for his mother kept him calm. His reply was "Ok." Now a new challenge, a stepfather, someone he saw as a replacement for his father. I know this drove him deeper in anger and despair. We are so proud of your efforts to influence the young man and choices he is making in his life. He continues to make bad decisions, but your efforts do not go unrewarded. Your encouragement has resulted in his continuing to pray to our Father each night before bed, regardless of where he is and what transpired in his day. He prays for safety and guidance through his turmoil and that his family will be whole again someday. Remember, the Father said, "Behold, I send an angel before you to guard you on the way and to bring you to the place that I have prepared" (Exod. 23:20).

Remember Hebrews 1:14: "Are they not all ministering spirits sent out to serve for the sake of those who are to inherit salvation?"

> Isaiah 30:21: "Your ears will hear a word behind you, 'This is the way, walk in it,' whenever you turn to the right or to the left."
>
> Briathos

Grace and peace be with you, Leuviah,

I see more darkness has befallen your young charge. Because he had no adult supervision and his recklessness, he had to move with his mother and siblings to the city. The location was truly the GHETTO! Despair and anguish upon arrival to the family's apartment was on his face. He looked upon a four-story dilapidated apartment complex in the ghetto. Trash was strewn all over the property. The building's dirty brick needed paint, and broken windows were in a state of disrepair. There were junk cars all around, no grass, dilapidated homes, and poorly maintained apartments. He walked into the complex to ascend to the third-floor apartment. His initial observation was of a horrendous smell of urine, mold, marijuana, and vomit. There were trash bags in the hallways and stairs. The halls were barely lit. Dark and dank, one could barely see down the hall. He thought of horror movie sets before the demons attacked. There was no elevator. Tenants had to walk up stairwells to reach their apartments. The noise from the other apartments included yelling, swearing, and screaming. His first thought was, "I have been condemned to hell." We felt much despair from those poor souls living in inhumane conditions. I know, Leuviah, you felt the despair and evil within these walls. My discussions with other guardian angels assigned to humans in the apartments confirm the anguish and despair of all those living there. In these sad conditions, many souls could be corrupted by demons and taken to hell to be devoured. The job of protecting and keeping souls away from the enemy is painful. Lyle considered running away and back to the streets. He thought, "Anything is better than what I just experienced." I could see the demons were working overtime to corrupt this young soul. The day a man was on the roof, shooting down at the people hanging and drinking near the local liquor store, was an awakening of just how terrible his life was becoming. He and his brothers and sister looked on in horror as events unfolded. Remember, before moving to the ghetto, they lived in a little country town, where everyone knew everyone. It was a quiet wholesome town. The family went to church every Sunday. The kids could play anywhere and find a safe adventure. Neighbors looked out for each other's children and would correct the kids as if they were their own when they did something wrong. This was no longer the case. Danger from drug addicts and continual challenges from other angry children resulting in bloody fights and gunfire was now the norm. I see how hard you are working, but there seems to be no peace for Lyle. He became angrier at the world and could be chided into fighting, causing great harm to himself and others. He was being drawn (by demons) to those persons who demons had corrupted to perform evil deeds. The demons were dreaming of the day his soul would be so corrupted that he could never regain a God balance in his life. Demons were discussing how his soul would taste as they devoured it at their table upon his death. I am an angel of God, and for one moment, the thought passed through me: how can this young person see any light to stay in God's light when exposed to this? It was you, Leuviah—your love and soft-spoken words kept him praying each night for deliverance from what he saw as the insanity of his life.

Keep charging. All will be well.
Briathos

My dearest student,

You are the embodiment of Christ's sacrifice and the Father's love. This is how I know you will do well in piloting Lyle through the negative influences in his life. I see the light shining brighter and some reprieve in his situation. The family moved into a middle-class home on the northern side of the city. I know! It is not the pleasant country surroundings where he spent the first fourteen years of his life but much improved circumstances. Now, not to say danger is all around, but you must be diligent! The enemy takes advantage of the calm to lull guardian angels into a false sense of security, and BANG! You lose Lyle to the dark side. Look at who he has chosen for new friends. This resulted in his associating with a group of men who had been to prison and hated those not like themselves. Remember the struggle you had when the group convinced him to jump into a van to attack another group. Two of the men, one in the passenger front seat and the other in the back had shotguns. The vehicle was driven by an apartment building, where a group the men hated hung out. I could see the demons smiling and whispering in the men's ears to shoot these men. As the van drove slowly past the building, they began shouting and scream evil, foul insults to the men inside. The driver said, "Now when they get close, yell 'Now,' and I will hit the gas. Then you two will open fire!" The men came running out to confront the insults. The man in the back of the van beside Lyle yelled "NOW!" He kicked opened the back door and began shooting, as did the man in the front passenger seat. It was dark, and all Lyle could see was flames spilling out of the weapons as the vehicle sped off. He heard bullets slamming into the building and watched people jumping to the ground or running in the opposite direction. His heart was beating out of his chest with fright. Lyle shouted, "Oh GOD! What have I gotten myself into?" Sweat was running down his head. As the van drove away, Lyle heard police sirens everywhere. He thought, "This is it. I am going to jail with these nuts!" This was the first time I had seen Lyle truly afraid and bewildered during the chaos. Leuviah, my sister, you whispered calming encouragement and kept him from taking a gun and shooting at the apartment complex. This could have been one of those life-changing events that drive humans into the arms of evil. They can bend the human mind to believe that evil is the only path. Your strength and love were the overriding factor that saved the day. I know there has been additional sadness in Lyle's life that will change his spiritual direction. Shortly after moving into the northside house, tragedy struck his family. This, I wondered, would crush this fifteen-year-old's spirit and drive him down a path of destruction. He had already participated in a shooting incident. We are concerned how far down the rabbit hole he may fall. Thursday, October 21, 1971 is a day that will stay with this young man for the remainder of his life. Late that night, there was a knock at the door, and his father's older brother and sister had arrived. The children were brought into one bedroom and told their father had been killed in an automobile accident that evening. The despair was palpable. The children's guardian angels were providing as much comfort as possible. Love and kindness was all that could be provided. There is little comfort for the anguish a child feels in that moment. As you reported, you could see the anger and pain in Lyle's eyes. There were questions as to why this was happening to him and his family. One would think enough is enough, but as we know, God's limits to pain and suffering is measured by that which a human can handle.

Well, as you said, this young man is the manifestation of strength and perseverance. I am aware he continues to pray to our Father each evening. He asks for forgiveness of his sins and that his brothers and sister will be lifted up out of the abyss of sadness. In view of these events, you need to encourage him to continue to pray. I foresee that he may wander from this effort, as his anger and inability to understand losing his father grows. During prayer the night after the notification of his father's death, Lyle asked, "God, why what have we done to incur your wrath?" We at the main office are concerned about his emotional state. He has not cried or discussed his father's death. He is turning this pain into anger, and we are concerned the enemy will use this to push him to evil actions. Although, I am encouraged by some of the recent events that have provided stability and love for him. He is still going to classes, although this is the third high school he has attended in the past year and half. Your creativity to place positive role models in his path to help where necessary is commendable. Take, for example, his history teacher. She saw through his hard exterior to see an intelligent, caring person that, with a little guidance, could be somebody. She provided a safe space in her classroom, even when her class was not where he was supposed to be. This kept him out of trouble. She took great interest in his goals and dreams, encouraging him to figure out where he was going and what he wanted to be. She convinced him to join the high school's baseball team. He not only made the team but was asked to play for the varsity. What a confidence builder. The teacher took him to dinner and the movies. She was the first person in a long time who provided adult guidance, encouragement where necessary, and scolding; someone who made him feel he had value. I know you observed, with some concern, as their relationship progressed, both of them appeared to have feelings for one another, more than mentor and student. You noted that the enemy was whispering to the teacher that there was no reason she should not be attracted to him. This was the case with Lyle too. We all could see feelings of love between them, but neither acted on that emotion. Look at when she was being harassed on the apartment intercom. Her ex-boyfriend yelled at her to come open the door, and he said "You need me. You open the door NOW!" Lyle saw the worry and concern in her eyes, knowing the ex-boyfriend would continue to bother her, even if he went away that night. Lyle saw the fear. His heart was beating fast as his anger began to boil over. He grabbed the apartment door and told her, "I will be back in a minute." Lyle opened the main complex door, where the boyfriend was standing. He rapidly closed the door behind him. Lyle looked at the man, saying, "You should probably leave and never bother her again!" The man laughed, asking, "Who do you think you are?" You reminded Lyle to be calm; he must settle this with dialogue and not violence. You pushed the demon away while he was whispering, "Hit him; he needs to be beaten!" Lyle grabbed the man by the front of his shirt and punched him in the face. Blood was everywhere. The man fell to the ground, got up, and ran to his car and left. Lyle returned to the apartment, and she asked what had happened. Lyle told her the guy would not be bothering her again. She hugged him tightly. They both realized during the embrace how great it felt, looked into each other eyes, and began to kiss passionately. Suddenly, they quickly pulled away, realizing they needed to stop. Leuviah, you and Mebahiah (her guardian angel) collaborated and influenced them that this was not what they should be doing, much to the delight of the main office. Great job dodging that potential mess. Fortunately, summer vacation began, and the teacher moved away to attend a master's program. In addition, his family moved to another city.

God does work in mysterious ways. Although these two humans became closer than you had hoped, the teacher's efforts to guide Lyle were beneficial. I could see a slight improvement in his approach to life. Hope springs eternal. Remember, sister, humans have both good and bad in them. It is the monster he feeds that wins the day, and with your guidance, a wonderful spirit will emerge.

Your loving teacher,
Briathos

Leuviah,

Just when everyone, including me, thought Lyle was turning the corner in his life, the family moved again; the fourth high school in two years. This can cause so much disillusion and anger. Couple that with the loss of his father one year ago, it could most likely be the catalyst for his anger and the trouble that followed. This was an opening for the enemy to weave his evil into Lyle's physic. He was not attending classes and causing disturbances in the class when present. The ugliest incident happened in the gym class. There was a spoiled rich kid jock in his class who had been harassing him for the past two days. It all came to a head when Lyle and the kid were playing on opposite teams in volleyball. The jock was yelling at Lyle, telling him, "You stink" every time Lyle made an error. Lyle's team was serving game point. As the play went on, Lyle's teammate set the ball. Lyle struck it and hit the jock in the face with the spike. Lyle was jumping with joy for the win. The kid ran underneath the net and began pushing Lyle and getting in his face. Leuviah, you did great keeping Lyle calm, impressing on him the incident was so ridiculous that it was not worth fighting about. Lyle said as much to the kid and walked away. The kid stormed into the locker room, cursing and screaming, "This is not the end of it." Lyle shrugged off the incident. As he walked into the locker, the kid was sitting on a bench by his locker, saying to Lyle, "You are a sissy for not fighting me. Afraid I will kick your butt." Leuviah, you kept him calm. As he walked away, the kid said, "Yea, you poor punk kids from the inner-city schools; most of you do not know who your fathers are." You could see the rage welling in Lyle. After all, his father had just died. The demons pushed you back, and with great glee, yelled, "Hit him! Smash his face into the lockers." Somehow Lyle remained calm until the kid jumped up and punched him in the face. The demons looked like raging beasts as they pressed each kid to destroy one another. Lyle's nose was bleeding, and he immediately punched the kid, grabbed him by the collar, and (as the demons were encouraging him to do) smashed his face into the lockers. The lockers had tabs protruding, and the kid's head was smashed into them. Blood was everywhere. Lyle let him go as blood flowed from above his eye and into his face. The gym teacher showed up, pushed Lyle out of the way, and provided medical attention to the kid. You did great keeping Lyle calm after this. The teacher ran to Lyle, grabbed him by the shirt, and yelled, "You kids from the inner city are all animals." Lyle said, "I did not start it." The other kids in the room confirmed Lyle's statement. The kid received thirty stitches in his head. I stopped reading the report, thinking this may be the breaking point. We were going to lose Lyle to the enemy. The past year had not gone well for Lyle. Two weeks later, Lyle, his mother, and stepfather met with school's assistant principal to discuss the matter. Unbelievably, his only punishment was that he had to apologize to the kid and his parents, pay the medical bill, and suspension for two days. Lyle was most relieved. He thought he was going to jail. As I observed this, I could see his anger was still influencing his decision. The real blessing was the assistant principal's compassion. He takes great care of his students, especially those with problems. He knew Lyle had lost his father and understood his anger. He was doing all he could to help the child. It was the assistant principal who convinced the kid's family not to sue or press charges. You know if they had done so, Lyle would most likely have moved to the dark side? His fragile state makes him a prime target for the enemy's conversion.

Pray harder to the Father for strength to get Lyle to the finish line and able to ascend to heaven.

Briathos

My honorable sister Leuviah,

Another year passes for these humans. It must be a relief not having had to save Lyle from dangerous ordeals for this past year. He is impulsive and can be easily pushed into participating in dangerous activities. I know he continues to pray each evening for guidance (although he never seems to hear the Word), looking for the path to serve the Father. Your report reflects he enlisted in the Navy and is planning to get married before leaving for his training. But just when you relaxed and thought he was moving in the right direction, working hard in school, and staying out of trouble, demons found a way to create chaos. Let me see if I have the event correct. Two weeks before graduating and one month before he was to be married, his history teacher from the old high school pulled into the driveway. She knocked on the door, and the stepfather answered. He greeted her with a smile and a surprised look on his face. The look was of concern and wonderment, why she has shown up after two years. He called Lyle up from the basement. Lyle walked into the living room. He saw her with her long blond hair and beautiful smile. His heart was racing; he was out of breath. She said, "Hi, you look wonderful." He and she walk rapidly toward each other, and with great anxiety, Lyle and Kathy (the teacher) collide, arms wrapped tightly around one another, expressing great joy. The embrace lasted longer than one would expect for friends. I know, Leuviah, you were concerned, wondering what she was doing there. You saw the demons' evil smirk, knowing he had something in the works to corrupt these humans. You whispered to Lyle to let go of the embrace and reminded him of his commitment to marriage. It overjoyed him to see her.

The demons were already plying their trade, encouraging Lyle to reconsider getting married, having him believe what he really wanted was Kathy. Demons were pushing his memories of the two of them to the forefront of his consciousness, reminding him of the fun they had together. The demons' goal was to sew despair and cause Lyle's emotional state to spiral down, possibly toward self-destruction. After a time, she ask him to go with her for a ride; she needed to speak to him. Lyle accepted but was curious about what was so important to discuss that could not be addressed now. Your comments in the report reflect the worry and anxiety you were feeling at this point in the conversation. He was very happy to see and be with her. He expected she wanted to catch up on personal issues between the two of them. Kathy seamed nervous as they left the house. I noticed the demons were laughing and knew something was amiss. They picked up some fast food from a local restaurant. Stopping at a local park to eat, they begin their discussion. Kathy started by telling Lyle, "I have thought about you often over the past two years, wondering how you were doing." She decided to find him, knowing he would be graduating soon. Lyle asked her how she was able to find him after the move. She said, "The only way was to contact some old friends who still worked at your old high school to get the address." Lyle smiled and said, "I am happy that you did." Suddenly, she averted her eyes from him and displayed a sad face before beginning to speak. Kathy said, "I really like you and wanted to see you for two reasons. First, as you can see by the bandages on my arms, the doctors have been drawing blood to try and find out why I have been so tired and sick. I finally received an answer. I have a rare blood disease that cannot be cured. The doctors say it can be controlled with medication and possibly give me ten to fifteen more years to live. Lyle, I was scared for some time, but now that I understand it, I am ok. So I have decided to be positive and take on my life. That is why I am here. I realize you are a great guy who I want to spend as much time with you as I can. I am finishing my master's degree at the university—so here is the deal—I have a great apartment, my parents left me loads of money, and I want you to come live with me. I have already smoothed the way for you to attend a university, and as long as we are together, I will pay all your expenses for school. I know what I want is you. Lyle's face showed surprise and a great big smile. He told Kathy he needed time to think about it; could he have a few days? Lyle told her he had joined the Navy and was scheduled to be married. He hugged and kissed her passionately. They drove back to the house and said their goodbyes. He yelled, "I will call you in a day or two. I am so excited to have seen you." Leuviah, I could tell, based on how you reported this, you were confused as to how this should be handled. Lyle was so confused about what he should do. He had never been one to confide in friends or family when personal crises occurred. Lyle went on long walks, muddling over his options, asking himself, "Do I really love the person I am going to marry? It is a great opportunity to go to a university and have it paid for." His thoughts drifted back to two years ago, reliving the exciting times he and Kathy had together. He loved her company. She came into his life when all seemed dark and lost with multiple moves and the loss of his father. It was truly DARK times for a young man. Kathy showed him love and that it was ok to not be angry at the world. For the first time in years, he had felt happy. The confusion continued. He thought he loved the woman he was planning to marry, wondering whether it was love or something else. He was excited about the adventures he would experience in the Navy. In great exasperation, he yelled out at one point, "OH GOD, WHAT SHOULD I DO?" Leuviah, this was out of your hands. You needed to step away from this decision. Human love is a quirky thing. Sometimes they see love based on lust, not true love. They live it in the heat of the moment instead of standing back and searching their soul for a better understanding of how they feel. You know this was the case with Lyle, as he is an energetic, impulsive soul. This is not a prayer God would answer. It comes back to that old free will the Father imparted on these humans. I know you want to protect him. What would be the right decision? Consider there are no sins being committed. He is not married to either one. He has committed to marry one woman, but there is no law God has to force him to marry. He is not fornicating with either woman. Most positive there is nothing the demons can do to influence the decision. They have nothing to gain. Lyle will make the best decision he can, based on all the facts. I see he is calm and organized as he is considering his options. This you can do: Help him to be calm and balanced as he moves through the decision process. Nice work keeping him on track. I know how easy it is for him to slide off the track and be pulled onto the wrong path. The demons almost fooled you into believing they had nothing to gain by the decision. This was not the case, as they were hard at work imprinting lustful thoughts in his head when considering the offer to go with Kathy. Keep reminding him the Father is the Truth and the Light!

Your mentor in Christ,
Briathos

Dear Leuviah,

I was glad to see Lyle had worked through his options and arrived at a decision. As I understand, it went something like this: He called Kathy to pick him up at the house. They drove back to the park for the discussion. When he jumped into the car, she could tell he was nervous. Her intuition warned her his decision would not be in her favor. Her heart was beating fast, in anticipation of a sad decision for her. It was all she could do to keep from crying in anticipation of the bad news. Lyle was quiet during the drive. Lyle's heart was also beating fast, and he was sweating, knowing he was to deliver bad news to Kathy. After they parked, he began to speak, with tears in his eyes, and he said, "I am sorry. I have made two commitments that I must see through. I do love you in my own way, but I must do what is right." Kathy started to cry, saying, "I understand your decision, but I am sad and disappointed. I love you and will miss you." They drove back to the house without a sound. After pulling into the drive with the vehicle stopped and tears in his eyes, he reached over, kissed her hard, and hugged her passionately. Kathy was crying, telling him, "I know I will never see you again. I hope you have a wonderful life. Goodbye." Mebahiah (her guardian angel) hugged her deeply, hoping to provide some relief for her pain. Mebahiah whispered, "All will be well, my love. God is with you."

Keep up the good work,
Briathos

Leuviah,

I see Lyle completed his training and has reported to his first duty station. It is wonderful news to hear you have connected with Kadkadael, the guardian angel responsible for Lyle's' new friend. You reported his name is Ron. He is a true believer in the grace of God. He and his family took Lyle and his wife under their wing, reintroducing the Lord to them. It is a credit to you, and your efforts paid off. It is a blessing to see God's light shining so brightly in Lyle. Your student now attends services Sunday and Wednesday nights and reads the Good Book daily, striving to be a better Christian. God is good. Be alert! I see more of the enemy's minions are present around him, enticing him with lustful and dishonorable thoughts. Consider the day he was carpooling with a coworker, who is also married. On the way home, the coworker drove to an apartment complex to visit another woman. While Lyle waited, the friend spent time in her bedroom. One can presume what events unfolded. This happened on a number of occasions. Once during the apartment visit, the women had a friend over when they arrived to "keep" Lyle company. The women and Lyle talked a great deal. Suddenly, she walked over to him, sat down next to him, talking while she caressed his back, saying how handsome he was and how she would like to have sex with him. She grasped his right hand and pressed against her breasts, saying, "Wouldn't you like to see more of me?" Lyle was blown away as to this aggressive move. She was a beautiful, dark-haired woman that most men could not resist. The demons were coaxing her, pressing her to entice Lyle to be with her. His demons were whispering enticements, "Look at her beauty, feel her soft, supple breasts, and smell her aromatic perfume." You could see he was giving into the lust. Suddenly, breathing heavily, Lyle jumped up and said nervously, "Sorry. I am married. This cannot happen." With his face flush and pulse beating rapidly, he yelled to his friend, "I will be waiting in the car for you." It was interesting to see the efforts demons made to entice him to commit adultery. Well, as usual, you were the positive influence that kept anything from happening. Your influence resulted in him deciding to stop riding with this friend. He knew that when one exposes himself to a possible compromising situation, it does not always end with a positive outcome. You are the shining light that will keep Lyle mindful of the Father and his goodness.

Keep the faith,
Briathos

Leuviah, peace be with you.

I see you are very busy fighting against the enemy. Lyle's new assignment in another country is exposing him to great danger, evil, and temptations. As you and the main office have noted, you see multitudes of demons running rampant with glee as they corrupt many humans in the towns and villages Lyle must work in. His continued exposure to alcohol, prostitutes, and exotic dancing may weaken his resolve. You must be ever so vigilant in reminding him he is a child of God. His shield must be bright and strong. Let us consider his exposure to death. That day he was riding with the local constabulary (Danny), who had just arrested a criminal for assault on Americans. He had stabbed and robbed a husband and wife. The husband received extensive damage to his arm, requiring emergency surgery. While patrolling with Danny, they saw the criminal in an alley, and Danny jumped out of the car and began chasing him down the alley to a dead end. He grabbed the criminal by the neck, threw him on the ground, and handcuffed him. As they walked back to the car, you felt the anger in Danny. He was screaming at the criminal. "I should kill you for making me run." The demon's eyes were displaying fire as he pushed Danny further, hoping for a killing; fresh meat for the nightly feast. Danny threw the criminal in the back seat and began an interrogation, more like torture. Danny was yelling at the criminal and was beating him with a pistol, imploring him to confess to the stabbing. The criminal was screaming, "You baboy (Filipino for pig). I will never admit to anything." Blood was flowing freely from the criminal's face, splattering everywhere as the beating continued. Danny became so angry that he pulled out his pistol and pointed it at the criminal's head, shouting, "You will confess, or I will blow your brains out." Spit was flowing out of Danny's mouth as he continued to scream, again striking him with the pistol. You could see the demons pressing the officer to shoot the criminal. You reported seeing the demons jumping up and down with excitement. They could see Danny was bending to their encouragement to shoot the "dirt bag." Both Danny and the criminal were shouting and struggling People could hear the shouting outside of the car as it passed them. There was so much chaos inside the vehicle, exactly what the demons wanted. You could see the rage in Danny's eyes and knew the demons were winning. Snarling and salivating, the demons were ready for death. Danny's guardian angel was doing all he could to provide calming words to his assignment. The criminal was smiling and laughing an evil gurgling laugh, saying, "Ha! I have nothing to say; shoot me. You will not do it!" All of a sudden, Danny raised the gun, pressing it right between the criminal's eyes. The criminal's eyes widened with fear, realizing Danny was enraged, and the criminal was pleading, "NO. DON"T SHOOT." Danny yelled, "You must die!" and pulled the trigger, killing the criminal almost instantly right there in the back seat. The gunfire was ear-splitting as it released its deadly shell into the head of the criminal. Blood splattered all over the back side window and onto the door frame of the car. The criminal's brains were slowly dripping down the back window. The demons in the vehicle were howling with glee; they had won a soul and would be feasting on it that night! I could tell, based on your report, the anguish you felt as the demons tore the soul from its carcass, all the time laughing and smiling. Did one of the demons actually tell you, "It is going to be a delicious feast this night"? It asked you, "How does it feel to lose another, soul?" Lyle continued staring blankly at the carnage that used to be a man's head splattered all over the back. He was shaking, pulled out a cigarette, lit it, and continued to look at the mess. He was stunned, not knowing how to react. A man's dead body lay in the back seat, with the back of his head blown out; the sick smell of blood and death. Danny calmly wiped off his gun and returned it to his holster. Lyle sat in silence as the vehicle drove to the local constabulary station, contemplating what had just transpired, and realizing for the first time since transferring to this country how dangerous it was. The body was unceremoniously manhandled out of the car and dumped in a bag for delivery to the hospital. Unlike America, the local constabulary can enforce the law as it sees fit. Reports were taken, and the incident was over. No charges were filed on the officer. In fact, he was praised for removing such an embarrassment from the world. In some third-world countries, the local constabulary has all the power. Unlike America, where justice is maintained differently. Leuviah, you did a good job calming Lyle and helping him understand this was out of his control. He is realizing his new world is the most dangerous place he has ever been. From a positive perspective, he continues to pray to God for guidance and safety. It must be rewarding to deliver his love and prayers to God. Unfortunately, in my experience, I feel this is only the beginning of more chaos for Lyle.

Brother Briathos

Leuviah, the shining light of God,

During these trying times of chaos for Lyle, as stated in the Talmud, "Every blade has its angel that bends over and whispers, 'GROW, GROW.'" This you must continue to do. It is time to visit Lyle in his dreams. You must show him the light and love God provides to protect him from the evil that surrounds him daily. The enemy is strong, but you, through the guidance and grace of God, are greater. Consider the challenge you encountered when he spent ninety days, in the jungle tracking an enemy for his government. You kept his spirits high, considering the conditions he lived in. Most of the time, the jungle was overwhelmingly damp with moisture encompassing his entire being. The humidity was so high that the jungle seemed to sweat water. There was the constant musty smells and living off limited food and water. The worst day came sixty days into this trip. You saw a demon acting more animated than usual. He was twenty feet in front of Lyle, jumping up and down, salivating, and screaming, "It won't be long now. I will taste a new soul tonight." Sensing something was amiss, as Lyle was walking and talking with another member, you whispered, "Lyle, change places with your friend." Lyle looked at his friend and said, "Hey, let me take the outside for a while." He changed his search pattern. This was an intuitive move. It must have been the friend's time to leave this world. You saw the demon swearing in rage, realizing Lyle would not be his dinner. He did smile, saying, "At least I will not go hungry tonight." As the two were walking and joking, suddenly, his friend stepped on a trap that decapitated him. Lyle froze, not believing what he saw was real. It must have been so distressing for Lyle to see his friend lose his head. The most unreal sight is when the body continued moving for an additional five feet before collapsing in a clump. The anguish experienced must have been unimaginable. You reported Lyle was screaming while holding his friend's body, asking, "Why did he have to die? How could God be so cruel to a young person?" I see the demons screaming with glee seeing Lyle's pain. They were encouraging him to question God and be angry with God for taking his friend. Demons whispered, "This is God's fault; he has no power here." I see Lyle's anger building, wanting to blame someone or thing for this death. The group leader grabbed Lyle by the front of his shirt, telling him to calm down and be quiet. The leader slapped Lyle a number of times to help him come to his senses. It worked. As reality returned, he came to the realization that if he had stayed on that path, it would have been him instead of his friend who died. This, my sister, must have been your greatest challenge, to calm him and keep him in God's light. When these events occur, the surviving member will experience survivor's guilt. Be on guard for this. It is commendable how you were able to encourage him to pray to God for his friend's soul. It angered the demons seeing him pray to God. This comforted you, knowing the young man who died was in God's grace as you watched his guardian angel gently lift his soul and guide him to heaven. The reaper was present to ensure the soul was taken in the right direction. Based on his life's efforts to be in God's grace, this was never in doubt. As for the demons, they were raging, running around, and howling, "No food tonight." The senior demon looked at you and said, "You cannot get them all. Watch out. We will corrupt your charge." As for Lyle, he is a strong, dedicated young man, and you must take care not to lose him to the other side. I am unsure as to what the Father has in store for him in the future, but you must keep him prepared.

Based on my archangel reports, this was only the beginning of evil incidents you and Lyle will be engaged in during his stay in the jungle. The week before the group returned home, chaos again ensued that should have changed Lyle's beliefs then and for the future. He woke early and noticed how beautiful the sunrise was. What a spectacular clear blue sky that day. I saw that you had visited him in his sleep, showing him the wonders of God and how beautiful the Father's love is. As the group walked to their designated patrol areas, the enemy was sighted, and a firefight began. I remember reading your observation reflecting on the number of demons that were with the enemy, smiling and encouraging them to KILL, KILL, KILL! The enemy obliged and began firing on the group. Lyle took cover. The firefight waged on for thirty minutes, with men falling on both sides. The demons were screaming with glee, knowing that there would be a great feast of souls at their master's table that night. As the men dropped, the demons tore at the souls, dragging them, kicking and screaming, to hell. Many of your brothers and sisters were present taking those souls in God's grace to heaven. It must have been a sight, seeing heavenly beings smiling as they lifted the souls up. You again managed to save Lyle from great harm, engulfing him with your wings as bullets flew all around him. You protected him. As bullets were flying, Lyle hid behind a crops of trees, firing as rapidly as possible. Suddenly, he felt a hot burning pain to the left backside of his head. Realizing he was not down and seemed to be ok, he continued to fire. The enemy broke off the assault and retreated. After the fight, the men gathered to care for the wounded. As Lyle sat reliving the chaos, trying to calm down, one of his team medical members said, "Hey, you might want to feel the back of your head; you are bleeding." He reached back and felt a wet warm fluid. He looked at his hand and noticed what seemed to be a lot of blood in his hand. During the chaos and adrenaline running through his veins, he had not noticed the wound. He called over the medic, asking him to take a look. It was a minor flesh wound that required little attention to clean and bind. Two days later, the group was relieved and caught a helicopter back to the primary operating area. Shortly after, Lyle was transferred out. Praise God for small favors. Leuviah, do not despair. All humans will receive injuries throughout their lives. Because of your protection, his injuries were minor.

Go forward with the grace of God.
Briathos

Dear Leuviah, guardian of man,

Turmoil appears to be in Lyle's path. This current assignment has and will put him in danger with the possibility of choosing evil over good. You must be mindful of this. To aid and forge your resolve in protecting Lyle, I wish to remind you of your many attributes. God has graced you with the ability to provide blessings, absolve transgressions, and bring grace to those assigned to you. You enable humans to be stronger, braver, and aid them to overcome life's challenges. This is how you keep this charge in God's grace, even during difficult times. He continues to pray each night, asking for grace and protection as he moves through his life. Let us look at his most recent life encounter. As part of his duties, while living in the Philippines, he was required to be on call to travel at a moment's notice. Assignments usually required catching flights at the nearby airbase. On this particular trip, he traveled by private driver to the airfield. It took three hours to get to the airfield. They were driving at night through the mountains. As you noted, this particular country's mountains lack lighting; even with headlights on high, it is difficult to see. While traveling from the south to the north, the driver informed Lyle that there were enormous bonfires in the middle of the highway and needed to slow down. The driver warned, saying, "In this particular area, armed communist rebels roam freely robbing, kidnapping, and killing. They especially are interested in Americans." The driver, being a local, instructed Lyle to fake sleep in hopes of dissuading the rebels from kidnapping or killing him. It was pitch black in the van. Lyle's heart was racing. As he lay there, he said a quiet prayer, asking God for protection. He began to devise a plan of attack, anticipating the rebels would attempt to take him for ransom or kill him. He was sweating profusely, trying to stay as still as possible. It was so silent that it amplified any noise in his head. Suddenly, the silence was broken when the rebels fired warning shots in the direction of the van. They were yelling in the local language, "Itigil" to stop. As the van neared the bonfire, Lyle realized the fire engulfed half of the road. He could see four men in front of the fire, yelling and firing their guns into the air. Lyle prepared to defend himself. He planned to take a gun from one of the men, hoping to survive and shoot any of the men who attacked. His adrenaline was pumping, fear of possible death kept him alert, knowing that there may be no other alternative. The rebels entered the van, yelling at the driver. They pointed two guns at the driver. He was pleading with the men not to shoot, as he was only a driver. They demanded to know who they were and where they were going. You provided a detailed report as to the angels with the rebels, attempting to calm them. The angels whispered in their ears, "These men are not dangerous," while trying to convince them to move away from the van. The demons were enraged, pushing the rebels to rob, kidnap, or kill the van's occupants. One rebel, who appeared to be the leader, walked with his gun raised at Lyle, asking in the local language, "Sino siya? Saan siya pupunta?" (Who is he? Where is he going?) Lyle remained silent and pretended to be sleeping. He thought, "Ok, this is it. If he steps any closer, I will have to take action. I will probably be killed, but I will not cower." I noticed in the report, you encompassed him in your wings, whispering to remain calmly, saying, "God will protect you." The driver stepped between the leader and Lyle, frantically speaking in the local language, saying, "We are no danger to you or the group. We are not worth killing or kidnapping." He told them, "If you do anything to this American, there will be nowhere you can hid from the full force of the US military." These words were enough to convince the leader that Lyle and the driver were of no value. The rebels released the van and sent them on their way. It was interesting to learn that Lyle said to the driver, "We both must have guardian angels with us. It is the only way we could have avoided being killed or kidnapped." They arrived at the airbase without further incident, and Lyle caught his flight.

I cannot believe that on the return trip, he ran into more problems again! Wow! How is this possible? The enemy must want his soul badly.

Crisis on the road—As I understand the events, his friend went north to pick him up from the airfield. While traveling at night, chaos arrived again! These roads are two lanes, running through many rice paddy fields, pitch black. One might almost think it is as dark as the entrance to hell. The local farmers' main form of transportation is carabao carts. Carabao are indigenous animals in the country similar to the African water buffalo. The beasts are slow but reliable to their life's task. They are primarily used for plowing the rice fields and family travel. To complicate matters, at night, the big rig truck drivers park on both sides of the road. This restricts the ability for north/south traffic passing through. It is so dark that one has difficulty seeing the road utilizing the car's bright lights. Lyle and his friend's vehicle were traveling south at eighty miles an hour, and suddenly, they saw a carabao cart in their lane. Both men yelled, "OH NO!" The driver automatically turned the car into the left lane in order to avoid the cart. Slamming on the brakes, the car swerved farther into the oncoming lane. They saw a big rig truck barreling down on them. You observed, there was nowhere to go! There were big rigs on both sides of the road blocking a safe exit. The cart was traveling slowly on the right, and the big rig was barreling down on the car.

Lyle was freaking out. He jumped on top of the passenger seat, screaming, "OH NO!" Fear welled up in him as he perceived they were going to be crushed by the truck or they were going to hit the cart and kill everyone in it. You must have been annoyed to see four demons on the cart laughing. They were hoping the car would hit the cart and kill all onboard. They were laughing and sneering with joy! They were waving at you as an invitation to come hit the cart. I see you took your best option and wrapped Lyle up, knowing he would receive some harm, even with your efforts. Demons on the hood of the car laughed with pleasure, salivating and pointing at Lyle, licking their lips, desiring his soul. The car swerved right, not wishing to hit the truck head-on, slamming on the brakes, and swerved left, then right again (skinning up the car), hoping to just miss the cart and avoid being killed by the truck. Holding onto the steering, keeping it on its last trajectory, the driver closed his eyes and yelled, "IT'S GOING TO BE CLOSE!" Lyle said a quick prayer, asking if this was his last day, God would take care of his family. He grabbed onto the safety handle to his right, closed his eyes, and waited for the end. There was a great crash. Amazingly, the truck smashed into the side mirror, sheering it off. Pieces were flying everywhere. Leuviah, I saw what you and Umabel (Lyle's friend's guardian angel) did. As the vehicle swerved to the left and right, the two of you strained to hold the vehicle in a line that would keep the car from hitting the cart and kept the truck from crushing the car. Losing a mirror is minor, considering what could have occurred. Outstanding work. I will tell you the main office was cheering as they observed this happening. The vehicle came to a dead stop in the middle of the road, just missing the cart. The guys sat there in the blackness with the headlights piercing the dark. It was dead silent. It was so quiet they could hear the cart driver leaving and yelling at them from fifty yards away. Both men sat in the vehicle, not making a sound for ten minutes. Once the realization hit that they had survived, each looked at one another and said, "WOW!" Not another word was said. The car was started, and they began heading down the road. Neither of the guys spoke for the two-hour trip home. I did see in the report that you were there praying to the Father to allow you to save Lyle. For the first time in this assignment and ensuing chaos, you believed that this was his time to be taken up to the Father. Because of your love and faith, Lyle arrived home safely. My primary concern is getting Lyle to again attend services in God's house. Hopefully after this close call with death, he will see how God works in his life. Leuviah, getting Lyle to attend services should continue to be the primary goal, more Word of God moves humans closer to the Father. I have communicated with Umable, congratulating for her part in protecting her charge. Guardian angels are wonderful beings!

Keep the faith. God is with you.
Briathos (your bother in Christ)

My dearest Leuviah,

Since Lyle has been assigned to the Far East, I have you challenged to be more proactive and imaginative in your protection duties. This includes improving his spiritual growth. As I outlined in your previous reports and acknowledged by the main office, Lyle has experienced many life-threatening dangers. Efforts by the enemy to corrupt and discourage him to the point of despair and movement away from the Father are severe. To compound the challenges, I see he has taken an interest in Buddhism. You confirmed this when you observed a devi (Buddhist guardian angel) hovering near him, whispering, "Buddha is the only true spree being. You will find peace and harmony you have so longed for." He visited a Buddhist temple. I can only imagine your surprise when you heard Lyle chanting "NAMO AMITUOFO" when meditating. This is a chant to develop inner strength when facing problems. I have no answer to your question: why can Buddhist devis take the form human form when working to convert their assignment? Your request to do the same is against the Father's guidelines; it will not be authorized. When it comes to guardian angels and their duties, the Father's plan is clear and cannot be deviated from. A few days later, you reported that Lyle had been meeting with a Buddhist monk expressing an interest in learning more about Buddha, temples, and how to meditate better. Through your diligence, you discovered the monk was actually the devi in human form. After Lyle left the monk, you went to the devi, asking, "What are you doing attempting to convert Lyle?" The devi smiled and said, "Buddha is the ultimate guide. I will do what is necessary to bring more souls to him." The devi changed back into its terrestrial form and left. So, not much success? On a positive note, during your conversation with the devi, the main office observed demons hissing angrily as they watched the devi speaking to Lyle, another force interfering with their efforts to corrupt him. As I understand it, he continues to pray to the Father but now is meditating and chanting as Buddhists do. There is more work to be done! You need to do more dream visitations. Show him the wonders of his Christian path that he should continue to walk, now and into the future. Remember, competition for human souls is not mutually exclusive between us and the enemy. There are other angels vying for the soul. We are the only holy entity that respects human free will (at our peril). Free will is a most wonderful gift given and a nightmare for guardian angels. We cannot interfere with their decisions, even when we know it may cause them to move away from the light and fall into darkness. We can whisper guidance and do dream visits to help guide them to the Father. When you communicate with Lyle, impress upon him that Buddhists do not believe in a soul. Leuviah, he is a wonderful young man searching for a firm footing in his life. He is desperately looking for spiritual fulfillment. He has prayed for help as he feels emptiness in his soul.

Briathos

Leuviah, my student,

Your efforts to keep Lyle on the right path are paying off. Let me see if I have this correct with how your last dream visit went. He was falling into a deep pleasant sleep. Lyle saw a beautiful sunrise with a glowing yellow orb, accompanied by a deep blue sky background. As he was standing in awe of this wonderful view, Lyle saw your silhouette coming out of the sun's glow. Lyle's expression was one of confusion and fear, wondering what it is that's coming toward him. He wondered how this was happening in his dream. He thought, "This is so real." He was dreaming, but his consciousness was alert to his surroundings. You walked directly to him and put your hands on his shoulders, saying, "Hello brother, God is good. I am Leuviah, your guardian angel. I bring you greetings from the Father. We notice you have been confused and searching for something to fill your empty soul." He replied, "I feel empty in my soul. I am searching for peace and happiness." You responded, "Know that my responsibility is to take all of your prayers to the Father and represent you to him to the best of my ability. We are concerned about you delving into other religions to find your answers. God is your answer, and through prayer, attending services, and living a godly life, your soul will begin to fill with joy and happiness. I am with you to protect and guide you to understand and appreciate God's grace. The Father gave you free will, enabling you to make all decisions without me able to intervene. I will be with you to encourage proper behavior that will lead you to the light." Lyle found his voice and asked, "Why should I believe that this is no more than a dream in my head?" You told him, "If you listen closely when awake, you will hear me giving guidance." Suddenly, Lyle's eyes lit up with recognition. He said, "I know you! As a kid, when I was being shot at and jumped into the water, I heard a voice in my head telling me to go down the dam, that I would be safe. As I slid down the dam, I saw an unusual light around me. I did not know what it was but felt safe as I traveled downward. It was you guiding me safely down and out of danger!" You said, "Yes, it was me, my brother. It is my job." Lyle smiled and thanked you for your help. He told you he would work harder to become more enlightened. You smiled and faded out of the dream. Lyle awoke the next day refreshed and had no recollection of your visit. That is how visitations work. His subconscious will collate the visit and form clear decisions, possibly improving his spiritual being. The good news is that information from archangels in the main office indicate Lyle continues to meditate. BUT when he is using the 108 Tibetan sandalwood meditation beads, instead of chanting Buddhist mantras, he says a prayer or positive affirmation to the Father. Nice work. The dream visit seems to have been of benefit. Leuviah, I have observed the challenges you have had to aid him in understanding ugly, evil events he has been part of. Consider his exposure to a man who committed suicide. As part of his job, he participates in investigations for the service. During a suicide investigation, Lyly learned the man was distraught. He had an affair while his wife was living in his home country. He had just been approved for a home and was bringing his pregnant wife to his duty station to live. I see his guardian angel Engel reported that he had done everything possible to convince the charge not to kill himself. His wife was coming that day, and he should have been happy. The day of the suicide, Engel saw three demons surrounding his assignment. They were pushing him to distress, encouraging him to pull out his gun and pull the trigger, telling him what he had done was unforgivable, that sleeping with another woman not his wife is an unforgivable sin; pushing him to feel the shame and sadness for his indiscretion. Engel whispered to him, "God loves you and would not abandon you in your hour of need." Engel pushed images of his wife and soon-to-be-born child into the man's mind, reminding him of their love. In the end, Engel failed, and the man succumbed to the enemy. On the day his wife arrived, he put a gun to his head, killing himself. His last words were, "I am sorry for my failure." It was an ugly sight watching the demons tearing his soul out from his mortal body with such glee. The demons looked at Engel with wild eyes, laughing and screaming. The head demon said, "You lost your soul!" We know whose soul they had at their feast that night. Lyle's thoughts were racing with sadness and anger, thinking and wondering why this poor woman had to experience such a horrendous loss. She had been so excited to see her husband after six months of separation. She sadly had to identify the body and take him home. Lyle wondered, "Why would God would allow this to happen, leaving a mother and child alone in the world?" You reminded him, "The Father gave the man free will to choose his destiny. The man had a choice and chose evil over good." My friend, there is evil, then pure unforgivable EVIL!

Another incident caused Lyle to question life and God's part in it. Consider the investigation he did with the woman who stabbed her boyfriend thirty-five times with a butcher knife. Look at how weak the woman's soul was to be driven to such a heinous act. The demons pushed her to a height of anger that she could not control herself. The victim was lying on his stomach watching TV, and she was yelling at him, "You have been sleeping with other women. I told you I would kill you." He yelled back, "Shut up. I have not done anything wrong." The demons were laughing, snarling in her ear, "He is sleeping with women each time he goes out of the house. KILL HIM!" She grabbed a butcher knife, jumped on him, and plunged it deep into his back, screaming, "You must die." He did not have a chance. She was jamming the knife into him with both hands, causing the knife to stick into the wood floor. Blood was everywhere. She was soaked in blood. The demons were insane with joy, rubbing the blood on themselves. Two demons plucked the man's soul out of the carcass, holding it by the legs, licking the torso, and disappeared into hell. One demon remained, softly whispering to the woman, "You have killed the person you loved. There is no reason for you to live. Your life is over. Kill yourself." She put the knife to her neck, and with one rapid motion, tore open her throat, exposing bone. Her blood squirted everywhere. In just a few minutes, she fell dead. The demon grabbed her soul, pulled her face to his, and screamed, "I will be eating you at tonight's feast." Her soul, realizing what she and done, began to scream in anguish and pain. We lost two souls that day, the woman's and her boyfriend's. As you walk with Lyle through this country and city, I see through your eyes the evil, debauchery, lust, and mayhem the evil enemy exposes him to. So many demons in one place must be a strain on you. I know Lyle prays for those souls who have fallen to such evil. We attribute this to your love and care for him. I know guardian angels feel a significant loss when they fail to keep God's children on the path of righteousness. Fortunately for all of us, we turn to the Father and receive his love. This enables us to stay the course. Keep vigilant as you are aware that evil is all around. We know that the enemy wants to consume as many souls as possible before the end of times. In the end, hell will fail and be destroyed.

Your guide in Christ,
Briathos

My dear Leuviah,

It is with great satisfaction that I see Lyle has left his current assignment and moved back to his home country. He and his family purchased a home and are settling in. The most encouraging news is that a local church member visited his family, sharing the Word with them. Lyle's family was invited to attend the service on Sunday. Leuviah, did you reach out to the local pastor's guardian angel, encouraging her to do a welcome to the neighborhood visits? Lyle and his family attended the service and met the pastor and congregation. Lyle and his wife were impressed with how the Word was being shared. When discussing the service with his wife, Lyle said, "I could feel the Spirit of God and the Holy Spirit in the church." They chose this church to be their home for worshiping the Father. I see they are now attending services twice on Sundays and the Wednesday service. It did not take long for the pastor to see God's light (thanks to your work) in Lyle and invited him to become a Sunday school teacher. We in the main office could see God's light growing in Lyle and his family. As I write this letter, I see the pastor asked him to become a deacon. The duties of the deacon include conducting church services when the pastor is absent. Your report reflects Lyle has been doing well at preaching the Word on Sunday. The main office acknowledges through your efforts and the grace of God that he is on a great path. WHOOOOO! Such a contrast from the previous few years. His Christian light is shining brightly. This is much better than all the previous dangers you and he have been through. Leuviah, look closely at Lyle. I see one of the seven deadly sins (pride) possibly creeping in on him. So young, given such a responsibility;

spreading the Word may be a challenge to keep his head straight and feet firmly on the ground. This is a most dangerous time for him. Lastly, I see many demons stirring around Lyle and his family, attempting to derail all the gains you have made with him. The most dangerous position for Christians is when they are closest to the Father and living a godly life.

Keep a watchful eye,
Briathos

My angel in Christ,

As I warned you in the previous letter, danger for Lyle to fall could happen. After he and his family moved to an upscale neighborhood near the beach, all your work started unraveling. It is interesting the subtle tools the enemy uses to move humans slowly away from a Christian life. Consider that his children were older and involved in competitive swimming. This required the family traveling each weekend to compete. Sometimes travel was required to other states, requiring the family to be gone for three or four days. So suddenly, there was no time for worship or attending services at the new location. Although, I know that when he first moved, the only church nearby was a charismatic congregation. It seemed all was going well. The family met new Christian friends. One incident caused him to doubt his faith. As you know, charismatic churches are high-paced and energetic in the worship services. Congregants yell and scream God's words, with some attempting to speak in "tongues." This can push members to be emotionally charged and sometimes lose control of their senses. During a particular emotionally charged service, his friend's wife was caught up in the moment. When the donation basket passed through the congregation, she put her grandmother's heirloom ring in the basket. As emotions calmed and senses returned, the woman became distraught realizing she had donated her grandmother's ring. She screamed, "I cannot believe I put the ring in the donation basket." Lyle and her husband told her they would figure out how to get the ring back. The ring had been passed down through the family for one hundred years. The men went to the church office to explain the situation and retrieve the ring.

Lyle and his friend went into the minister's office, asking to speak to him regarding a donation. They were invited into the minister's office. He inquired, "What can I do for you, gentlemen?" Lyle spoke up, telling him about the ring being donated. He said, "My friend's wife had been overcome with emotion, praising God during the service. She was not thinking clearly about the family's sentimentality behind the ring. She put the ring in the basket as a donation." The church minister and staff told them, "The ring was a gift to God. We will not be giving it back." Lyle screamed at the minister, asking him, "What kind of a man of God are you? Have you no compassion for one of your congregates?" Lyle grabbed the minister by the jacket. While shaking him violently, he screamed, "You are not a man of God! You are an evil human being." I see you were in his head trying to calm him but to no avail. Suddenly, he struck the minister several times, telling him, "you are a demon!" Of course, there were demons screaming into Lyle's ear, "Hit him. He is evil and should be punished by you." Lyle and his friend stormed out of the building, yelling, "What kind of God allows these types of crooks to represent him?" It is interesting that the minister did not call the local police to arrest Lyle for assault. Well, as we learned a few days later, the minister had been arrested for fraud. He had bilked many parishioners out of thousands of dollars. This drove Lyle from attending any church, weakening his spirit and relationship with the Father. We in the main office sadly heard him speaking to his wife, saying, "I cannot trust anyone who speaks of God and religion. How can God allow this to happen? I see why there are people who do not believe." The demons took advantage of this. They pressed him to forget the guilt he felt spending weekends traveling with his children swimming instead of being in church. I know you did all you could to encourage him to continue attending. It was a nice touch to remind him that there are evil people misrepresenting the Father everywhere. As days moved on, I see he and his family were getting further and further away from a Christian life you had helped develop. You saw the demons sneering at you with much joy as they worked to guide Lyle away from God. Well, it seems you are back to the drawing board to fix this. Keep the faith. Lyle will turn toward the light.

God is on our side. You will win.
Briathos

Dear Leuviah, I hope this letter finds you in good spirits.

Just when I thought your task could not get more challenging, you reported Lyle has a new assignment to a staff of fourteen working for an admiral. This requires taking battle groups to sea, conducting training, and deploying for six months or more to various parts of the world. I see this may cause strain in his family's relationship. Based on the last reporting, challenges have already began. The ships got underway in route to the Persian Gulf. The battle group pulled into an island between the Atlantic and the Straits of Gibraltar for a short liberty for the crews. Lyle went ashore with his mates. Instead of visiting tourist sights, he went to the local bars and began consuming large amounts of alcohol with his friends. Isn't it discouraging to see so many demons in these establishments, coaxing men to drink mass quantities of alcohol and cause trouble? These men have been traveling for some time and needed to relieve the stress through alcohol consumption. Most times, the result is mayhem, fights, and incarceration for many of these men. I know all of your brothers and sisters present do all they can to minimize violence, a monumental task. Back to your pupil. What was he doing when he ran out of the bar, jumped headfirst into a cab, and disappeared from his friends? The next morning, I see he was nowhere to be found on the ship. His boss and friends were concerned about his well-being. Well, as you reported, he woke in a cow pasture with cows all around him mooing. He was disoriented and surprised, not knowing where he was and how he got there. You did your best to protect him through the night, ensuring no harm came to him. As he lay there, I know you left him to check the Book of Life. You wanted to make sure this was not his time to be taken to the Father. My, how many times in his young life have you had to double check the Book before providing protection to him? You got him moving. Not knowing where and how far he was away from the ship worried him. He walked through a pasture to a dirt road. Lyle had no idea what direction he should go. You whispered, "You should go toward the sunrise. The ship is anchored on the eastern port of the island." Your suggestion gave him the resolve to go east. As luck would have it, a horse-drawn hay wagon was going in that direction. He stopped it and asked the man where he was. The man started speaking in Portuguese. The island is part of Portugal. The principal language is Portuguese. Fortunately for you and Lyle, the man spoke English. Lyle said to the driver, "I am heading east to get back to the port where my ship is anchored." The man began to laugh a loud belly laugh. It seems that your student had somehow traveled seventy miles from the port to end up in the farmer's pasture. Completely baffled, he asked the driver if he could direct him to a phone to get transportation back to the ship. The man said, "I am traveling to the port to deliver supplies to the locals. You are welcome to ride in the back on the hay." Unbelievable! Seventy miles. It took all day riding in the back of the hay wagon to get to the pier. Once he arrived, Lyle thanked the man for his help and offered him payment. The driver thanked him, saying, "It is enough payment listening to you try to figure out how you had traveled so far away from the ship." Lyle jumped down from the wagon, stretched out his stiff body, and headed for the ship. Upon entering the ship, he went directly to the admiral's cabin to report his return. The admiral was very angry. He told Lyle, "YOU ARE RESTRICTED TO THE SHIP FOR THE REMAINDER OF THE PORT VISIT!" The admiral had sailors combing the local community for his missing staff member. Wow! Not a good look. You may consider a few dream visitations. Remind him of his loyalty to God and how important his relationship is to the Father. Show him how foolish he looked excessively drinking and lying in the cow pasture. The demons assigned to your pupil must have been busting with joy to see this transgression. These are trying times, and you need to be ever so watchful. His will is being bent to the darkness.

Keep the faith,
Briathos

Dearest Leuviah,

As the main office reported, the Azores incident was minor considering the events that occurred in Palma Mallorca, Spain. As I revisit the incident, do not blame yourself; his free will determines the actions he takes. You are doing your best to keep Lyle moving in the right direction. So, the ship had been traveling from the Atlantic Ocean and into the straits of Gibraltar, stopping in Palma for a visit. The first days went well. You guided him to visit the local tourists attractions. Nice job emphasizing visiting the old cathedrals, hoping to reinforce the richness of his faith. He even attended services at one church. On the evening of the second day in town, his friends convinced him (with the pressure of demons) to go to a local bar to "unwind." A demon said to him, "Remember the fun you had in the Azores drinking and laughing with the crew? Remember how much fun it was to retell the adventure of waking in the cow pasture and riding the hay wagon back to the pier?" Lyle chuckled remembering the adventure. While in the bar, he was enjoying time with the crew, and a local Spanish woman came to him and struck up a conversation. During their conversations, a local man walked up to the woman, spewing insults because she was associating with the Americans. In a drunken slur, he yelled, "Why are you interested in this American pig? He is ugly and stupid-looking!" You forcefully whispered, "Just walk away." The woman said to the man, "You are the pig. He is just a nice man." To the joy of the demons, the man struck the woman, and mayhem ensured. Lyle grabbed the man by the shirt and struck him twice, knocking him to the ground. The entire bar erupted into a brawl. Bodies flying, chairs flying; there was chaos everywhere. In the end, the local authorities handcuffed Lyle and other offenders, arresting them and throwing everyone into jail. As Lyle sat in jail, demons were sneering at you, laughing with exuberance, and taunting you. They were laughing, saying, "We have won another round in corrupting Lyle's soul." With a bowed head, you looked at Lyle with sadness and disappointment. Well, the admiral himself showed up at the jail. Lyle jumped up when he saw him, anticipating being released from his prison cell. Although he knew the admiral would be angry, at least he would be out of the cell. That was not to be, as the admiral said to him, "I could have you released into my custody, but I will not. You will spend the two-day sentence in this jail. In addition, you must pay a $200 fine for your part to repair the bar. As one of my staff, you embarrassed me and must pay the price." Lyle dropped his head with shame, knowing he had lost the respect of the admiral. As he stood there, fear rushed through him, realizing he would be spending two days in the cell with criminals. Let me see if I have your description of the conditions in that cell correctly. There was filth and dirt everywhere and a toilet in the center of the room to be used, where everyone can observe a person using the facility. Ten other men were sharing the cell, none who could speak English. Many had been arrested for violent crimes. The stench was overpowering; no showers or place to clean up. The food was sparse and not very good. Demons were everywhere, stirring up the evil. They encouraged men to attack Lyle, the dirty American. With a coordinated effort between you and other guardian angels in the cell, you were able to keep everyone calm. Lyle was safe. The demons had been battling you for Lyle's soul for so long that they were doing all they could to destroy him and his spirit. They gnashed their teeth, telling you, "We will win. Someone in here will beat your charge." For the next two days, Lyle was on his guard. He managed to make friends with a number of his cell mates. This provided him protection until his release. Two days later, he was released to the Navy and taken to the ship. To your relief, the admiral restricted Lyle to the ship for the remainder of the port visit. I heard his prayers over the next few days, asking God to forgive him for his transgressions. Maybe something good did come from this incident? Leuviah, Lyle has committed one of the seven deadly sins, gluttony. His excessive use of alcohol could fall into the category of gluttony. You must convey to him this is what he has done. Hopefully, this will be at the forefront of Lyle's mind before he engages in this type of behavior in the future. I know you will work to help him refrain from repeating this. No, you do not need a vacation! This soul is your assignment, and failure is not an option. You are doing well; keep the faith. All will end well. God's will be done.

Remember, God will not give you any more than you can handle.

Briathos

Dear Ariel and Daniel,

I see you took advantage of the opportunity to observe and learn techniques Leuviah uses protecting her assignment. Giving you access to Leuviah's experience should aid when you receive your first human soul to protect. Leuviah's charge is a very challenging soul to protect and keep on God's path. Consider the Dubai affair after his group entered the Persian Gulf for assignment. The first three months, the group spent patrolling international waters. The primary assignment was to protect oil tankers from being attacked by the belligerent country that started a war. Shortly after, the admiral gave his staff a one-week vacation in Dubai. This allowed the team to rest and relax after a prolonged patrol. Lyle is an adventurous soul, and he took time to visit local sights. He dined at the same local mutam (restaurant) each evening. Three days into his vacation, while eating at the mutam, a tall, beautiful, dark-haired, almond-eyed, sensuous Persian woman walked up to the table and introduced herself. With a beautiful smile, she said, "Hello, my name is Aghigh. It means precious and rare." His first thought was, "I have never seen a more beautiful, sensuous woman in my life. Hmm, precious and rare is a fitting name." Leuviah impressed upon him that lust was in his heart. Wow! Another of the seven deadly sins. He invited her to dine with him. Aghigh ate dinner and visited with him for some time. Time seemed to stand still. Not only was she beautiful but intelligent and witty. They discussed the local sights he had visited and laughed at the differences in each other's customs. She asked him, "Have you ever seen camel races?" He replied, "No, do people really race camels?" She continued, "In two days, there will be a great camel race in the desert. Would you like to see the races up close and personal? If you wish to go, I will pick you up at your hotel in the morning." He had some reservations about going. Although, based on the look in his eyes, he was going to go. According to Leuviah's comments, her wings were bristling, thinking there was danger in that invitation. Not only because of the woman's beauty and his attraction to her, but she also thought this might be a con to get him into the desert and rob him. Leuviah spent the better part of the next day trying to dissuade Lyle from going. Even a dream visit could not convince him not to go. I did observe the dream visit. Let me describe Leuviah's efforts. After spending the day with Aghigh, Lyle went to his room and quickly fell asleep. As he began to dream, Leuviah came to him out of the darkness, wings fully open, and glistening in white. He smiled and said, "Hello, Leuviah. Why are you here again in my dream?" She replied, "I am aware of your desire for Aghigh. Considering her beauty and charms, I understand, but you must remember you are married, and it would be a sin to lay with her." Lyle laughed and said, "She is one of the most beautiful women I have ever met. I understand your concern, but I have no passionate desires for her. Yes I want to spend time with her. I am lonely and just want some female company." She looked at him and said, "Lyle, I am worried. I know you humans are weak and can falter. I will leave you now and pray that your intentions remain pure as you have said. Peace be with you." Well, he went. Aghigh picked him up, and they traveled for two hours. During the drive, he saw nothing but sand dunes and desolation. I knew Leuviah was trying to figure how she was going to be able to help him if trouble occurred. She contemplated, "If he is left in the desert, might he die? How can I help him?" The demons were enjoying the chaos, hoping that the worst would happen, and Lyle would die in the desert. Two demons in the car were smiling. One chuckled and said, "We might be feasting on this soul this evening." Leuviah reminded the demons that if Lyle died, his sins were minor, and he could do penance and be forgiven. She would escort Lyle to the Father. This enraged the demons. They were scheming, figuring out how they could corrupt Lyle sufficiently to cause him to fall. There was this beautiful woman they were going to use as bait. Remember, he has not seen his wife for the past four months. It was the perfect opportunity to coax Lyle into adultery. As you will find out, humans are flawed and susceptible to their feelings. This is most prevalent with lust. In those weak moments, they are vulnerable. If they were not so flawed, guardian angels would not exist. As the vehicle sped down the road, just over a rise, Lyle saw the most amazing sight: white tents as far as the eye could see, right in the middle of the desert. All of the white contrasted beautifully against the brown desert. It was spectacular! They pulled onto the desert, heading for the tents. Upon their arrival, Aghigh took Lyle to one of the tents where there was a feast and food from all parts of the world. The food included goat, goat eyes, lamb, and beef. There were some unusual vegetable dishes Lyle had ever seen. He was definitely out of his environment. He planned to try everything. He did not want to offend the sheikh. Aghigh introduced Lyle to the sheikh, who had organized the race. As it turned out, the sheikh was Aghigh's father. After eating and drinking all they could, he watched the races with great zeal and excitement. There was betting on the races. Lyle, with encouragement by the sheikh, picked out a camel to win for the sheikh. Lyle's camel won. The sheikh smiled, patted Lyle on the back, and said, "Ha, beginner's luck." As the day went on and night fell, Lyle realized they were to stay on the site for the night and travel back to town the next day. Leuviah saw the demons dancing with excitement. They thought it was their time to corrupt Lyle with lust. What better way to achieve this than with a beautiful woman dressed in the local garments, attending to all of his needs? The demons were encouraging the woman to entice Lyle and convince him to share her bed. With the help of alcohol, the woman's beauty, and her aromatic perfume, demons went to work. They put visions in his head, showing him lying with her in his arms, and ravishing her through the night. Aghigh took him to the tent where she and he were to sleep. As he walked into the tent, there was a huge main living area, cushions, and chairs everywhere. To his left were separate sleeping quarters with shades blocking each sleeping area. Leuviah was doing all she could to plant the seed of guilt for even thinking about bedding the woman. Demons planted visions in both their minds, showing them together in the same bed. Lyle pushed the images out of his head. After closing the front tent flap, Aghigh said, "Your sleeping quarters are here." She opened the curtain and pointed in the room. She said, "Or you can have this." She disrobed, saying to him, "I want you to be with me tonight." I know all of you were shocked by how wild the demons were screaming and dancing with joy, knowing not many men could resist such a woman's charms. They were whispering in his ear, "Lyle, look how beautiful she is, her smooth almond skin, twinkling eyes, and her suppleness. Take her; she desires you! No one would know but you. Smell her rich aroma, and feel the pounding of your heart. Feel the passion and desire building in you. What joy you could have this night." Leuviah pressed hard in Lyle's mind, saying, "This is not who you are. You are on God's path. Do not stray in a weak moment." As you both know, he found the strength to tell her, "You are one of the most beautiful women I have ever seen, but I cannot lie with you. I am married and loyal to my Christian vows." Aghigh said,

"Lyle, although I wish to have you ravish me, I understand and respect your wishes. I would like to remain friends and hope that once we depart, you will write to me. If some day you are no longer committed to another, I would wish to be her replacement." She turned, closed the curtain, and walked to her sleeping area. Amen to his strength and Leuviah's efforts. This is an example both of you will need to keep in mind when caring for your assignments. Remember, when it gets too difficult, you have God's love and support to lean on. The demons were enraged, screaming in anguish for their failure. Leuviah noticed a third demon appeared. It was beating the two demons responsible for working to corrupt Lyle. They were taken to hell, and the demons' souls were served to the others at the feast of souls. Satan and his minions eat their own when there is failure. This was a sad sight for Leuviah. The two of you must take all that you have learned. This will aid you when guiding your humans. Angels receive blessings from God and have empathy even for demons. God is love.

Your loving teacher,
Briathos

Dear Leuviah;

Thanks to you for allowing Ariel and Daniel to observe your work. They learned a great deal about human behavior. Both came away with a better understanding of how challenging the job will be to ensure their assigned humans stay on the right path. Ariel observed that lust seems to be one of the most challenging of the seven deadly sins to steer humans away from. Her observations with the beautiful Persian woman cemented in her the understanding how difficult it is to be a guardian angel. Great work thwarting the enemy from winning that round. I see in your report the lengths you went to protect Lyle from danger. Let use recap the most current chaos.

While back on patrol in the Central Persian Gulf, he attended a morning meeting with his boss. During the meeting, there had been discussions about a force from the belligerent country planning to attack a special forces team assigned to two barges in the north. He wanted a member of his staff to volunteer to go as a communications liaison to the barge. This was to ensure accurate real-time information collected would be communicated to the admiral. Well, of course, adventurous Lyle volunteered. They transported Lyle via helicopter to the barges the following day. The first few days were calm, giving him time to adjust to barge living and become acquainted with the team assigned to monitor and protect the north. All that was soon to change. Oh, most amazing, with your reminder, he continued to pray every evening. The third day began as routine as all others. There were a couple of small boat patrols, exercise, meals, then relaxing before rack time. That day there was a beautiful full moon. It lit up the night.

Around 8:00 pm, Lyle was standing near a sailor manning the 20mm chain gun. Water was calm with barely a ripple, peaceful. The full moon shining on the water appeared as a ball of light. Suddenly, both men noticed unusual water movement, as if a boat were traveling in the barge's direction. You noticed the demons on the barge jumping and cackling with glee, as if they knew something sinister was going to happen soon. One looked at you and said, "It is time Lyle died. We will attempt to take him to hell for dinner this night." You became alarmed and raced to where Lyle was standing. You whispered, "Watch to the North; something is happening." Suddenly, machine gun and small arms fires erupted from out of the darkness. Tracer bullets lit up the night sky. The gunner near Lyle returned fire and took cover behind sandbags. Lyle was in the open; the sandbags were too far away. He dove down on the deck. It was the best he could do. You whispered, "Jump into the water. It is the only safe place for now." I see you wrapped him in your wings to protect him from the bullets as he jumped into the water. Because of your quick thinking, he was untouched by the gunfire. While in the water, he yelled to one of his team mates, "Hand me some grenades." What was he thinking? You encouraged him to get back on the barge. Instead, he began to swim toward one of the assaulting boats. Because of darkness of tnight and gunfire, no one on the enemy boat heard or saw his approach. He swam next to the boat and grabbed onto the left side. As he pulled the grenade pins, he pulled himself up the side of the boat and threw the grenades in the center and began to swim away. He was not able to get far enough away when the grenades exploded, engulfing the entire boat into a hell fire. As Lyle was swimming away, he felt the concussion of the explosion and was knocked unconscious. I know you thought this was the end of him, especially when you saw the demons hovering and salivating over him. They yelled, "If he is unclean, we will be feasting on his soul this night." You went to him and held him, saying, "My brother in Christ, this is not your time. Hold on; they will come." The demons were enraged, screaming, "You are taking our feast!" You yelled back to the demons, "This soul is in God's graces." The firefight lasted around thirty minutes. Lyle's amazing efforts directly contributed to the attack ending. The team on the barge realized he was missing, launched zodiac boats, and rescued him. Until then, they did know who or what caused the explosion on the enemy's boat. Once the crew was back on the barge, Lyle was awake, examined by the medic, and cleared for duty. This team of sailors were SEAL team members. They were impressed with Lyle's heroic performance during the chaos. They made him an honorary member of SEAL Team Two, presenting him with a Trident (symbol of the elite fighting unit). As usually happens during a firefight, chaos ensues, and no one had reported to the admiral as events unfolded. No further incidents occurred during Lyle's stay. One week after Lyle's arrival on the barge, he was air-lifted back to the admiral's flag ship. Leuviah, you are a shining example of what guardian angels should be. You communicated and guided your charge and made him safe in a time of crisis.

God has blessed you.

Your esteemed colleague,
Briathos

Leuviah, my dear;

Lyle is in a dangerous place, requiring you to be ever so vigilant with his well-being. I read reports from two of your counterparts discussing protecting their charges from a ship explosion. This happened when a mine was placed in its path. Without the help of your brothers Jeliel and Sitael, you might have had to get another protection assignment. Losing a charge is disconcerting. I would like to review your efforts by revisiting the incident. The assignment given to the admiral was to take his nine-ship task group into the Persian Gulf. They were to provide protection for his country's flagged oil tankers. There was a war going on between two belligerents, with many battles happening in the Persian Gulf. The admiral's job was to ensure the safety of his assigned oil tankers. A belligerent had threatened to sink any oil tankers transiting the straits on their way into the Arabian Sea. The goal was to choke off all oil being shipped around the world. The straits link the Persian Gulf to the Arabian Sea for further transit around the world. This would have caused economic disaster for many countries, including the admirals. Lyle's group was patrolling the Central Gulf, monitoring radio traffic, specifically monitoring the progress of one of his ships returning from escort duty. Escort duty is when the warship travels with the oil tanker, providing protection until it leaves the straits. The last report received communicated that the ship had transited the straits and was heading north to its patrol grid. Suddenly, the radio came alive with a distress call from the escort ship. "Mayday, mayday! We just hit a mine on the aft port section of the ship. We are taking on water. The after section of the flight deck is three fleet above the waterline." Being fifty miles away from the explosion, the admiral sent a helicopter ahead to access the damage. Upon arrival, the helicopter radioed back, "This is November Foxtrot One, I can confirm the mine exploded on the aft port side (left back of the ship). The ship is taking on water and doing all it can to stay afloat." The admiral grabbed the radio and immediately ordered the three ships in his group to "jump to flank speed and get to the sinking ship as quickly as possible." Arriving on scene two hours after the initial call, the admiral was able to visually access the situation. He could see the ship had smoke billowing all around and crew members running on deck. Other warships stood off while they established communications with the mined ship's captain. The admiral radioed all ships in the vicinity, saying, "This is Task Group Alpha. Stand off 1000 yards from the ship until the area has been checked for additional mines." You could see the aft portion of the ship where the mine must have hit. The helicopter flight deck was a few feet above the waterline. Crews were busy moving injured members close to the helipad to enable a quick extraction for medical care. Others were being loaded onto small boats for transfer. Ships were launching helicopters to bring the wounded and excess supplies off to lighten the load. Organized chaos bests describes the situation. It was interesting to see so many demons watching and waiting for deaths to see if the souls could be taken to hell. Many guardian angels were working diligently to save their charges. Jeliel (guardian angel) reported that his charge was trapped below deck, and he had a broken back. The compartment was flooding, and there seemed to be no way out. With the exception of a red emergency light, there was little light in the compartment. The sailor was praying; he thought this was the end. Despair was evident. The young sailor prayed harder, "Please Lord, give me the strength to swim and find my way out." There were demons telling him, "You are not going to make it. Give up." He was moaning in pain, thinking, "I am not going to make it. Lord take care of my family." Water was almost over his head. Fear consumed him, driven more so by the demons. The enemy looked at Jeliel with a twinkling eye, yelling, "He will be mine!" He laughed a horrific laugh of joy. Jeliel, with great effort, continued to provide him with hope that he would survive. He had a broken back, but with Jeliel and the grace of God, he pressed on. Jeliel coaxed him to keep moving. He whispered, "Everything will be ok. You are safe. Believe God will save you." The compartment rapidly filled with water. In excruciating pain, he swam underwater, striving to find an exit. He was running out of air and began to panic. Suddenly, he saw a glowing white light at an emergency exit. Jeliel's encouragement gave him renewed strength. He quickly swam toward the light, the light that enabled him to find the hatch and open it. Leuviah, it was Jeiel who provided the guiding light, helping her charge get to the exit. As the hatch opened there, the sailor saw Lyle smiling and saying, "It is a miracle you were able to find the way out." Lyle saw the deck below was dark and full of water, and he asked the sailor, "How did you manage to find the hatch in the darkness?" The sailor kept saying, "I did not feel alone. It is as if someone or something had given me the strength to move and helped me find the hatch." He said, "The feeling happened right after I prayed to God for help!" I congratulated Jeliel for a job well done. I am to understand that Lyle volunteered to helio over from the flag ship to provide assistance. There were many dangers there. The ship's after section, where the helicopter pad was, had sunk so that the deck was just three feet above the waterline. You could see water splashing on the deck. Fortunately, it was a sunny, blue sky day with calm seas, making it easier to keep the ship afloat. The battle to keep the ship afloat remained in question. Communications reported that the crew was doing all they could to keep the ship afloat, but it was not certain that their efforts would be fruitful. Consider where Lyle was, on a ship, three decks below a ship that hit a mine, not even his ship. He went below as part of a rescue team. As they entered the compartment, the water was filling the space, with smoke everywhere. It would be easy to get lost below deck under these circumstances. The team he was assigned to found and saved other sailors in that compartment, directing them to the hatch that would take them to safety. The smoke was so thick that it became difficult to see which direction they should travel. There were some red emergency lights providing limited visibility. It was a fog-like light but did not provide sufficient light to be sure which direction to travel. Sailors were beginning to panic as smoke filled the space. Water was still rising from the space below where they had pulled out the injured sailor. What to do? You and Jeliel provided the calm the sailors needed to remain focused. Their guardian angels whispered to them which direction they should travel to escape this danger. Oh my, the enemy was working hard, causing confusion, saying to the sailors, "You are going in the wrong direction. You are going to die." You held Lyle's hand, providing encouragement that all would be well. Through the chaos and smoke, a ladder leading up to the next level was seen. Lyle yelled to the others, "This is the way out." Upon reaching the next level, Lyle saw a Damage Control team coming toward them. The team provided additional breathing masks and directed them out of the ship. The Damage Control team managed to stop the water leaks and put the fires out. When the main deck was reached, the injured sailors were laid in a basket and transported to another ship for care. You and the other angels saved many sailors under your care that day. All angels provided the calm necessary to guide the charges out of danger. It did not hurt that Jeiel provided a small celestial light near the hatch. I can only imagine how angry the enemy's minions were. I see they were jumping up and down, howling, "You angels foiled our attempt to kill humans. We will not give up." I do know that some of those who failed were summoned to hell for their own form of judgment. As they entered hell, they were put on the menu for the soul-eating feast. God teaches us love. I was sad to hear about the minions' demise. God loves all of his creatures, even the demons. Outstanding job! I fear this is not the end. Reports indicate that Lyle's boss had been directed to devise a plan to punish the belligerent country responsible for the mining. The demons were overjoyed to see all of the rage spoken by the humans. Many desired to KILL other humans. I fear a sad day is forthcoming. Remain on guard. This may tax your spirit.

Go in God's grace,
Briathos

Leuviah, I hope this letter finds you in good spirits.

After watching the chaos you just experienced, I wanted you to remember that the Father's love will shine upon you always. I see that after the mining incident, plans were devised to strike back at the offending country. The admiral and his staff, including Lyle, transited twenty miles from the Northern Gulf to the straits. The team transferred to a waiting ship for further travel. They jumped on the ship's helicopter for a fifty-mile flight over the Arabian Sea to an aircraft carrier. The admiral and his staff had developed a comprehensive attack plan to be executed upon approval by the commander of the Middle East forces. They spent all day explaining the plan and discussing what resources would be needed for proper execution. I saw the look of sadness and disgust on your face as you observed the excitement the demons were displaying. Leuviah, I know you were calculating the number of deaths, wondering how many lost souls the demons would devour. The enemy was busy whispering to the men, "Make sure you exact your pound of flesh from the belligerent country's military for the mining." I could see the anger grow in those men's eyes, discussing expected enemy casualties. This was joy for the demons as they sharpened their knives, preparing for extracting the dying souls for their feast. As night fell, the briefing concluded. The admiral and his staff were to fly back to the straits, where a ship was to rendezvous with them for transportation to the Central Gulf. The staff was to travel in two helios. As Lyle stood on deck, he commented on how beautiful the scene was; the full moon glistening off the calm seas, and a slight breeze blowing to mitigate the Arabian heat. What a peaceful sight. He said, "Helio night flights are so cool and exciting with a pitch black sky; the only light is a shining moon." That was not to last. Lyle's helio launched from the carrier deck with three staff members, pilot, co-pilot, and one air crewman. Well, as you know, all was to change quickly. The helicopter was about five miles out from the carrier when it began a small but noticeable port to starboard pitch. The pilot radioed to the carrier, saying, "This is Bravo Six Alpha. We are having some rotor pitch problems. We are returning to the carrier." Lyle, now fully alert, knowing the helio had to travel five miles back to the carrier with serious engine problems. Knowing there may be a problem, he began thinking through his helicopter training. If the helicopter crashed in water, his first thought was, unlike the training, which took place in a pool in daylight, it was night. It was pitch black, and as he looked around to find the red emergency light over the nearest emergency exit, it became surreal to him. The only lighting, besides the red emergency exits, was those on the control panels in the front of the craft. You could see shadows of the other men and could feel the palpable anxiety, all hoping the helicopter could limp back to the carrier. As the helio banked for the return route, a high-pitched sound could be heard from the rotor. The entire craft began to shudder and drop altitude. The pilot radioed, "MAYDAY! MAYDAY! We are not going to make it back. We will have to ditch!" He radioed the craft's longitude and latitude coordinates. Lyle's heart began to race, and his thoughts became muddled. His first thought was, "Oh crap!" Just then, the helio began a slow-spinning descent. You quietly said to Lyle, "Be calm. God is with you. Remember your training." The spinning caused disorientation as Lyle tried to maintain focus on the emergency exit. He knew the first goal was to survive the fall and impact. With blackness all around, he was unable to discern when the helio would hit the water. Were they falling from one hundred feet, fifty feet? Lyle wondered, "Will I survive the crash?" He said a couple of prayers, asking for strength to get through the panic he was experiencing. Lyle quickly thought through the survival steps from training in his head. First, survive the crash; second, wait for the helio to pitch over and begin to sink before releasing from the seat (this was to ensure when exiting the craft, he would not get caught in the rotors); and third, finally get to the nearest exit, then to the surface. You did a good job keeping him focused on the task at hand. All of a sudden, crash! The helio hit the water. Lyle was surprised by the impact. For a split second, he froze in the dark, in his seat. The impact took his breath away. His mind was jumbled, his thinking was slow, and everything seemed to be in slow motion. You prodded him to get moving. The helio filled rapidly with water. The feeling of the water brought him back to focus. He remained seated waiting for the roll. In a panic moment, when the water was filling the craft, he realized he could not see how fast the craft was filling. He worried, thinking, "When should I take my final breath? I need to time my release from the harness as I take the last breath and break for the emergency exit." His heart was pounding as he practiced gulping air in preparation for his last breath and hoping for escape. It suddenly dawned on him. "I have no idea how deep the helio sunk. Will I have sufficient air to make it to the surface?" Leuviah, you whispered, "One thing at a time." The water was quickly rising. He could feel it rising, waiting for the right moment to take his last breath. The craft rolled on its side, sinking quickly. When he felt the water neck high, he gulped as much air as possible just before being completely submerged. He reached for and released the harness. Seeing the red emergency exit light, he quickly swam toward it and out of the craft. As he left the helio, he realized he could not see anything. There was nothing but blackness all around. Lyle was unable to determine which direction was up. He swam away from the craft and hovered in place, unable to determine up from down. Panic was overcoming his scenes, realizing he could not hold his breath forever. The demons near him said, "Give up. You will fail. You will not make it to the surface alive." He could not figure out up from down. His panic intensified, causing more confusion. He thought, "Which way? I cannot even see my hands. What should I do?" Just as the demons told him. There you were, reaching out to him, suggesting to break his training rules, reminding him God loved him, and whispering, "You should release the CO2 canister that inflates your life vest. As the idea came to his consciousness, his eyes lit up with hope. A thought came to him. "Well, I have no other option." He released the canister and began to rise. He swam as fast as possible, knowing he was running out of air and had no idea how far away the surface was. Nothing but blackness, he could feel his lungs tightening, knowing that the oxygen was being depleted, and soon his body's reflexes would demand and gasp for air. His heart beat hard against his chest. His head pounded under the pressure. Demons were doing their best to convince him to give up, telling him, "You are not going to make it." One of them screamed in his thoughts, "GIVE UP! YOU ARE GOING TO DIE!" Leuviah, you would not let him quit, telling him, "Quitting is not an option." He felt as if his eyes were going to burst out of his head, beginning to panic, thinking, "This is it. I cannot hold my breath much longer." All of a sudden, he burst through the black surface, gulping huge quantities of air, panting, and grateful to be alive. With the realization he had made it, he looked around, wondering if there were other survivors. As his eyes adjusted to the darkness, except for the shining moon, which was a Godsend, he saw white flashing lights in the water. Each survival vest contained a white strobe light that was activated by saltwater. He could see four strobes near him. The pilot began to call out, "If you can hear me, swim in my direction." Once all were together, it was realized that there was one crew member missing—the co-pilot. Everyone called out, to no avail. Demons must have been happy believing one person had died. The pilot could see the light from the helio and decided to dive down to get his co-pilot. He asked for a volunteer. You tried to convince Lyle not to volunteer. But you know his mantra: "experience the experience." He and the pilot dove down to the helio and grabbed the co-pilot. The pilot realized they were running out of air and motioned Lyle to let go of the co-pilot and swim to the surface. He refused and grabbed the co-pilot's CO2 canister and pulled it. Since the pilot and Lyle were holding the co-pilot, all began to rise rapidly, broaching the surface. The aircrew member who was a medic swam over to assess the co-pilot. Realizing the co-pilot was unresponsive, he began procedures to revive him. He did his best performing chest compression. Considering they were in the water with no hard surface to place the co-pilot on these efforts were monumental. After much effort, the co-pilot was breathing. He received a gash on his head that rendered him unconscious. It was bandaged. He was doing as well as possible. It was almost funny to read how angry the demons became. They were not able to cause a death and consume a soul. There were six men floating in the Arabian Sea, and it was so dark that they could barely see their own hands. The only light was provided by the moon and the flashing strobe lights. Lyle looked at where the carrier was, realizing it was so far away, and he could only see it as a pint-size light where it stood. I know the men were scared, and someone asked if there were sharks in the Indian Ocean and, of course, there were. I could see the panic in the men's eyes. Here they were floating in an ocean, feet dangling like so much chum, wondering if they would feel a bump from a shark just before they were devoured. Some of the men joked about feeling like the men of the USS Independence, The WWII ship that was sunk in the Pacific and had lost 180 men to sharks, devouring them as they floated in the dark, waiting for rescue. Their biggest fear: sea snakes. Sea snakes were prevalent in these waters. One bite would kill a man in five minutes. The demons were dancing on the water, laughing, and discussing how they could steer sharks or sea snakes toward the humans. You and the other guardian angels were busy keeping their assignment as calm as possible. Interesting, one of the crew was a Buddhist, and his devi was there protecting him. The pilot was his charge. That Devi did a great job protecting him. While floating in the warm, dark waters, the pilot knew the capacity of the helicopter that would be rescuing them. He devised a priority plan, deciding who would be loaded first for transportation back to the carrier. The craft could hold two additional passengers. With six people, there would have to be three trips. The travel time from the carrier to the wreck site would be about fifteen minutes one-way. A round trip was thirty minutes. Accounting for the additional time to unload the passengers, the pilot estimated forty-five minutes for each trip. This meant that the last two members picked up would be in the water an additional 1.5 hours. He said he would be one of the last and looked for a volunteer. Lyle spoke up, willing to stay to the end. The co-pilot was one of the first to be saved. The next two included the air crewman and staff member. The next day, the staff was flown back to the Gulf to meet with the nine ships' commanding officers. This briefing outlined the attack plan. Leuviah, maybe you do need a vacation. This assignment is keeping you on your toes. There must be something the Father has in store for this human; so many close incidents with little more than scratches. You are the primary reason for his safety. Remember to keep reminding Lyle that God is with him. He should desire to improve his relationship with the Father. Based on what we know about the attack plan, you are going to busy keeping him safe. Stay with him, and remind him to keep praying at night as he does. I know his prayers lately have focused on thanking God for saving him from the near-disaster helicopter crash.

God bless you,
Briathos

My sister Leuviah,

You did well protecting Lyle in times of combat. Everyone at the main office, including Archangel Michael, was rooting for you to succeed in protecting during the attack. I know all guardian angels present were saddened seeing the death and destruction. Your faith and love of God keeps your spirits high, enabling you to console and guide Lyle. After the helicopter incident and subsequent return to the flag ship, I see all ships and Special Forces teams were briefed on attack plans. The ships were assigned to specific task units. Three ships to each unit, with a unit to the north to attack the enemy's land-based units; Central unit was assigned to hunt two ships that were involved in the mining incident, and South to take out enemy aircraft and one transport ship. The ship was used as a launch site for enemy small boats that attacked and boarded oil tankers. The admiral's staff were split between the three task units. Lyle was assigned to the Central task unit as communications liaison between the unit and the admiral. The admiral took command of the South task unit. As the morning began, Lyle monitored the surface radar. Reports came over the radio from task unit 3 in the South, reporting that they had encountered high speed small boat gunfire and were engaging. Carrier aircraft were providing air support and had shot down a number of enemy aircraft. Suddenly, the radar watch yelled, "I am picking up enemy ship contact bearing 230 degrees from our position. I cannot narrow down the ship's exact location." Lookouts could not see any ships in the direction reported. As quickly as an eye blinks, the radar operator screamed, "Missiles inbound!" Seconds later, the lookouts in a loud excited voice screamed, "Ship barring 230." The ship had hidden behind an island, steamed out just before firing multiple missiles at the three ships in task unit 2. I noticed you instinctively moved closer to Lyle. Lyle radioed the admiral and reported, "Sir, we have enemy missiles inbound, baring 230 degrees." Tensions were high in the Combat Information Center. It is interesting to be closed in a room, unable to see events unfolding above deck. Many thoughts moved through Lyle's mind. "What if we get hit? What about my family? Could I survive the attack?" What a fine job you did infusing a pleasant thought that if he did die, God loved him, and he would be with the Father this day. He knew that many missiles glided along the surface. When in ranger, pop up, and strike the target. Others struck at the waterline, possibly breaking the ship's keel, increasing the likelihood of sinking. There was organized chaos in the Combat Center. Men yelled as the missiles rapidly closed the distance to strike. Crew members reported, "All hatches are battened down." This action mitigates the danger of sinking when/if the ship is hit. The commanding officer had directed all ships to release missiles on the target. Pandemonium erupted in the ship's missile bay. The men responsible for loading the missiles for a retaliation strike had loaded two different missiles types on the rail. This caused the missiles system to fail. Missiles must be the same type in order for the firing system to function properly. Lyle was watching the radar, observing the closing speed and direction the missiles were moving. He quickly realized two missiles were tracking directly at his ship. He said a small prayer for everyone's safety. The captain sat calmly in his chair, tapping his hat on his thigh, asking, "Are we going to get any missiles away before we are hit?" Some of the younger sailors were visibly shaken as they considered the possibility of a missile striking the ship and killing them. The demons were salivating with glee. They pointed at individuals, identifying those who might die, who were ripe for consumption at the evening soul feast. You observed your colleagues doing their best to calm their assignments. The ship's missiles were finally released at the target. The sound of the ship's Close In Weapons System began to fire. This is a radar-operated gun, firing 4,000 rounds a minute, saturating the inbound missile air space with bullets in an effort to destroy it before it hits its target. Lyle could hear men yelling on deck, seeing the missile smoke trail, and all knew impact would soon occur if the defense did not work. Seconds later, over ship wide radio, the order was given to "Brace for impact." This is a warning to take cover because the missile(s) were going to strike! Lyle's heart was in his throat. His initial thought was to dive under his console for safety. He thought to himself, "What is the use if a missile hits us? More than likely I will be dead." He said a small prayer to protect not only himself but the crew. Leuviah, you wrapped your wings around him in an effort to provide as much protection as possible. As did the other guardian angels. As I envision the scene, angels covering their charges, demons jumping up and down, anticipating the missile strike and carnage, and the crew diving for cover. Lyle observed during the chaos how different each person reacted to the warning. Some jumped under equipment, others stood at their station working holding on, others crying for their mothers, and some invoking God to protect them. The anxiety was so intense, and you could feel it throughout the Combat Center. As all waited for impact, the ship's Close in Weapons System (CIWS) guns continued to fire. The whirling of the bullets firing from the CIWS was unmistakable, even in the confined Combat Center. Suddenly, there was a great explosion heard off the port side, causing the ship to shudder. No one knew if the missile had struck the ship or the defenses worked. Shortly after the explosion, great cheering was heard from outside of Combat. The Bridge reported that one missile had been shot down, another missed, and the third was thwarted by one of the other ships in the task unit. Great loud cheers broke out in Combat, releasing the tension in the room. The commanding officer yelled to the group, "Settle down. I want a report on the missiles we fired." The radar operator who had been tracking the missiles abruptly yelled, "Missile strike on target." A helicopter was launched to assess the damage. You had already known the shot was successful. The demons were wildly leaving the ship, heading for the ship that had just been hit. You heard one cheering, shouting, "We have to collect those souls. let's get our dinner!" The helicopter flew by the ship, reporting that the super structure was burning in the forward section. There were survivors in the water. The pilot requested boats be launched to pick them up. The commanding officer reported to his central commander the results and requested to close for collecting survivors. To the astonishment of Lyle and many others, the order came down for the task unit to close within one quarter of a mile and sink the ship with deck guns. These are mounted cannons shooting large shells. I heard the other angels were visibly shaken by what they heard. Prayers were said for those who may be alive, but not much longer. As the ship was sinking, you could hear the demons' HOWLS of joy. God protect those souls. With disgust and sadness, you watched the event unfold. Lyle went to the Bridge to observe the action. He went to port side and watched through the "big eyes." These are huge binoculars that can see for long distances. Before the shooting began, he observed the black smoke billowing from the entire front of the ship. Flames were flickering everywhere. He could see what appeared to be men in the water struggling to stay afloat. He wondered how scared these men must be. The three ships began to fire their main guns at the burning ship. Shot after shot hit the ship piercing the hull followed by explosions. After about ten minutes, the firing stopped. He looked through the binoculars and saw a terrible sight. The forward portion of the ship was blown away. In his amazement as he watched, the ship pitched forward and began a downward decent into the water. Within minutes, the ship had disappeared with a last great belch of water. His first thought was, "Oh my, how many families would be missing a father, brother, or son by the end of the day?" The horror you observed was almost too ugly to watch. The demons were extracting those souls that were destined for hell. The souls were howling for mercy and help from God. As you know, it is not our place to save a soul after the human shell has died. These souls, in God's eyes, had committed sins that could not be redeemed. We still prayed for those souls, for we knew the agonies they were going to experience. The helicopter flew over where the ship was last seen, looking for survivors. He reported that after the gunfire, there were no survivors. His report was almost overwhelming. For all those guardian angels present during this sad incident, this can serve as a reminder of what will happen to Lyle or other charges' souls if one fails at their task. It is known that after stressful incidents, especially when humans are involved in taking other lives, guardian angels need to be vigilant for those in their care. Humans tend to become depressed as they process the men's lives they participate in. Some humans have been known to take their own lives. Watch the demons closely! They have consumed many souls this day and are looking for weaknesses that can be exploited. Protect your charges from depression and contemplation of suicide.

God is with you. Stay the course.
Briathos

My sister in Christ,

I see Lyle and the staff have transited from the Gulf and are heading home. I am sure this is a great relief to you with him being out of combat danger. While transiting toward the Suez Chanel, Lyle displayed how compassionate he can be to others. En route, the ship pulled into Djibouti, Africa, to get medical x-rays for a sailor who had been injured on the ship. After the ship moored and secured the lines, the injured sailor was taken to the local medical facility. While on deck looking at the land, Lyle thought, "This is the most desolate and depressing place I have ever seen." There was nothing but sand and a few huts with humans wandering around who looked more like skeletons than living humans. Most were malnourished. This was obvious; their large protruding bellies, sunken eyes, and were so thin that it appeared as if the skin was hanging on bone. Such a look of anguish on these people's faces. The sight caused Lyle to look away in sadness and disgust. A thought occurred to him, "How can God allow such suffering in this world?" When a ship pulls into port, they off load all of the trash they stored on board during the transit. It is against international law to throw trash into the sea. Ships hold all their garbage until they pull into a port. The ship's crew collected and loaded a truck with all the garbage collected for the past month to a nearby dumpster. The crew drove to the dumpster and unloaded the garbage. Even before they threw all the trash bags into the dumpster, out of nowhere came these thin, bloated-bellied people running straight to the garbage dumpsters. There must have been fifty sad-looking gaunt humans rushing to tear open the bags. They grabbed old food, rags, anything they could carry. It was so sad and sickening. Lyle prayed for some kind of relief for these poor souls. As he stood looking at these barely human people fighting over the ship's garbage, Lyle had an idea. He ran to the admiral's food pantry and filled a trash bag with fruit, canned goods, and vegetables. He also found some canned spam. As he approached the ladder to exit the ship, the sailor on watch held him up, asking "What is in the bag?" Lyle replied, "It is the admiral's trash." The duty sailors assumed the bag was trash and waved Lyle on, allowing him to disembark the ship. As he stepped down from the ship's ladder, he noticed three small children hiding behind a wall. He realized they were too small to compete with the others at the dumpster. Lyle walked to where the children were hiding, opened the bag, and offered the children the fruit and vegetables. At first, they were too shy to take the offering. With a warm smile and soft voice, Lyle said, "It's ok. Here, take what you want; you look hungry." The children gently accepted the bag. With their big hollow eyes looking at Lyle, they gave him a great big smile and ran off. As Lyle walked away, he looked back and saw the children disappear into a little grass shack. A little girl step out of the shack, waved, smiled, and disappeared. Lyle was so happy; he is one of those souls who love children and will do anything to help them. Leuviah, you should be so happy. All the work you have done to keep him close to God is paying off. No greater gift can one give of themselves than charity. He will never know what fruit this act of kindness may bear.

God is with you,
Briathos

Dear Leuviah, one with the challenging task,

You reported Lyle's battle group has transited the Suez Canal and is now anchored in Haifa, Israel. He has been on liberty for the past ten days, staying at a local hotel. Being an adventurer, he struck out on his own to see the local sights. Every morning, he sits at the same local café in awe of the beautiful view. The café overlooks the Mediterranean Sea. As the sun rises over the horizon, the yellow orb reflects off of the water, appearing as a celestial light. This was a wonderful respite after the chaos experienced in the Gulf, for you and him. I see your respite was short-lived. On the second day in Haifa, while sitting at his usual table admiring the view, a beautiful, tall, slender Israeli woman walked over to his table and introduced herself. She said, "Hello, my name is Eva. What is your name?" Lyle said, "My name's Lyle. Would you join me for coffee?" She sat down next to him and asked, "Who are you, and what brings you to Haifa?" He told her he was on vacation from the ship in the port. He discussed how he enjoyed the old architecture and churches in the area. She asked, "If you are interested, I could show you around the city to more than just the tourist sights." Leuviah, I know you were hard at work reminding him of his family obligations. Eva was so beautiful and charming, and Lyle could easily lose his way. The demons were in his head, telling him how beautiful she was. They pushed images into his head showing Lyle and Eva embracing and kissing. She was so beautiful, she might have been an angel. Her perfume was intoxicating. He pushed the lustful thoughts out of his head. He did accept her offer to show him the sights. For the next three days, she showed him all the exceptional sights, and he met some of

Eva's friends and her family. He told Eva he had wanted to see the diamond mines and purchase diamonds for his wife. He had purchased gold in Bahrain with a plan to purchase diamonds in Haifa. Lyle was going to have a ring made for his wife and necklaces for his daughters. Eva took him to the mines and introduced him to the owners. She was able to negotiate an exceptional price for the diamonds he selected. They had great fun going through the mines looking at how diamonds were being extracted, cleaned, and processed. They had breakfast at the café each morning and used it as a jumping-off point for sightseeing. On the fourth day, as they were sitting in the café, she suggested they should take a trip to Jerusalem to see the Wailing Wall. You pressed him to say no, knowing how vulnerable Lyle was. This could be trouble. Adultery is a most terrible sin that comes with the added pain of guilt. This guilt destroys the offender and families. He told her he was very excited to go, and she was the perfect companion. You thought that since he agreed to go, you would lose that battle with the demons. The demons looked at you with their antagonistic smirk, believing they were going to win this soul that night in all places, JERUSALEM! Eva suggested they travel by bus, spend the day sightseeing, and get a hotel for the night. He agreed. You were thinking that although he was spending time with the woman, you felt his character was strong, and with loyalty being so important, he would not succumb to a lustful weakness. The bus arrived in Jerusalem early afternoon. When they went to the hotel to register, he asked for two rooms. He said, "You are one of the most intriguing, beautiful, and desirable woman I have ever met. I cannot contend with my conscience if we stay in the same room." She said, "I understand. I really enjoy your company and would love to have you always as a friend." I almost laughed when you described how the demons were screaming, pulling their ears, and swearing. Fear was seen in their eyes remembering they had already reported to their head demon that adultery success was going to be happening that night. Your instincts were correct, and he would not allow lust to fog his judgment. I know you saw the friendship the two humans were developing. And friendship is what it would be. The two had a wonderful experience. She educated him on all things Jerusalem, temples, the Wall, and the customs associated with the Wall. On the bus ride back to Haifa, the two were enjoying discussing the day's events and the great time that was had. Suddenly, out of the darkness, gunfire was heard, and bullets were hitting the bus. All of the passengers were trying to get as low as possible on the bus. You should have realized something bad was going to happen. Just before the attack, the demons were jumping high in the air with glee. They knew there was going to be an attack and wanted those souls. You covered Lyle with your wings, whispering, "Get out of the bus's emergency door." With his heart in his throat, ducking bullets, and eyes as big as the moon, Lyle grabbed Eva and crawled along the walkway of the bus. As they exited the bus, they ran into a field and took cover. Bullets were flying everywhere. You could see the path where the bullets where heading as the tracers lit up the sky. It was a terrorist attack on the bus. One man who must have been the leader, yelled, "You must turn over any Americans to us. If you do, no one will get hurt." The men were shooting and walking toward the bus, anticipating getting hostages they could take with them. With the help of the darkness, everyone from the bus hid themselves in the field. As suddenly as the initial gunfire began, suddenly gunfire was heard and seen coming from the opposite direction than the assailants. A firefight ensued. Men yelled in pain from bullets striking them. Tracer bullets flew everywhere, lighting up the night sky. Just ten minutes after the second gunfire began, it was over. The silence was deafening. Lyle and all the bus riders heard someone yelling in Hebrew. "You can come out now. All is clear!" Eva explained the man was part of the Israeli Defense Force, and it was safe to go back to the bus. After all of the bus riders were checked out by the IDF medical staff, they were allowed to get on the bus to complete their travel to Haifa. It must have been disturbing watching demons attacking those souls who had lost their lives during the IDF firefight. Demons where so angry that there were few souls to torment. They were particularly ravenous with those souls they took as they Gnashed their teeth, screamed, and gnawed at the poor souls. You said a silent prayer. The bus arrived in Haifa at 2:00 am. As Lyle walked Eva to her apartment, the day's events were discussed attempting to make some sense of the attacked. Eva said, "It is a blessing and a curse to live in Israel." "The blessing is that I am Israeli and live in a beautiful country. The curse is because of the strife between two people who are biblical cousins. Maybe someday both sides will come to understand this and peace will prevail." Lyle reminded Eva, "This is my last night in Haifa. I will be heading back to the ship tomorrow afternoon. Will you meet me once more at the café?" As they stood at her apartment door, she smiled and said, "I know, and yes. Are you sure you do not want to come up?" Lyle replied, "No," kissed her, and said goodnight. The next morning, they met at the café for coffee and discussed the events of the past few days. He said to her, "I hope you realize under different circumstances, I would have pursued a relationship with you. You are a dynamic woman that any man would be proud to have as a partner." Breakfast was finished in silence as each contemplated the exciting adventures they had. Enjoying the beauty of the day and the pleasant company, they exchanged addresses and said they would write. It was time for him to get back to the ship. Eva walked him to the ship and said a tearful goodbye. So, let's see, just when you thought there would be some modicum of calm, he tangles with a woman and is attacked by terrorists. I guess it is all in a day's work for you, my friend. God chose the right guardian angel for this soul. Based on the Book of Life, you have fifty-six more years to guide and protect this human. Keeping him on the right path has been challenging. If it were easy, anyone could do it.

Keep his path as straight as possible.
Briathos

Leuviah, my sister;

Has it really been one year since Lyle returned from his deployment? We have noted no challenging incidents in your reports. Reestablishing his relationship with his wife and kids is wonderful. He appears to be happy. As I write this, I see he is again underway, heading for another six-month tour in the Gulf. It is interesting to learn he has been corresponding with Eva, who he met in Israel last year. Human love is a tricky thing. They tend to feel an intellectual or physical attraction that could be love. In most cases, it is lust. Their weakness creates difficulties in their lives. Your report reflects, based on his correspondence with her, he has established a genuine friendship. In one of her previous letters, she wrote she had joined the Israel Defense Forces. Knowing the dangers the IDF encounter each day, Lyle worried about her safety. It has been four months since her last letter. The ship was underway, and mail was spotty at best. Lyle justified this to account for the length of time since Eva's last letter. He also figured Eva was busy training and might not have time to write. As Israeli citizens, all are required to serve in the IDF for two years. Her duties began five months ago. Two months into the cruise, the ship pulled into the Haifa, Israel, port. Lyle was very excited to get off the ship and go visit Eva. He took a couple of days leave, wanting to spend time with Eva and catch up. Leuviah, you already knew the sadness he was about to experience. As he neared Eva's apartment, excitement rose in him, anticipating seeing her. Lyle jogged the last couple of yards. He called out "Eva" as he knocked on the door. A man unfamiliar to him answered. Lyle ask if Eva was home. The man said, "I do not know an Eva. I have been living here for the past three months." Lyle thought, "Oh what a bonehead, of course she would have had to move." They assigned her to patrol in Jerusalem, where there had recently been unrest. He remembered where her parents lived and jumped into a cab, directing the driver where to go. When he knocked on the door, the mother greeted him with a sad smile. He smiled back, anticipating seeing his friend. As Lyle looked into the mother's eyes, anxiety rose in him, realizing something was wrong. Even before he asked, the mother became very somber. She asked him into the house. As she started to speak, tears were rolling down her face. Eva's mother said, "Two months ago while on night patrol, Eva's team came under gunfire. During the firefight, Eva was shot and killed." He felt great pain while attempting to comprehend what he just heard. "OH MY GOD. This cannot be happening." Lyle grabbed onto Eva's mother, holding her, crying, and saying, "I am so sorry. Eva was such a wonderful person. Why do bad things happen to good people?" Leuviah, you already knew she had died. You engulfed him in your wings, consoling him. You whispered, "She is safe and happy and is with the Father." You could feel the staggering anguish Lyle felt. As your words filled his thoughts, he angrily thought, as if talking to you, "It is not good enough that she is safe and happy. She did not deserve to die!" More work for you, Leuviah, to help him sort this out. It is difficult to find true friends in a human's life. He will miss her. He asked Eva's mother if he could visit her grave. The mother gave him directions. He hugged her tightly, expressing his sorrow and left. Nice job soothing his sadness as the cab drove on. Arriving at the cemetery, it did not take long to find her grave. He stood there sobbing with sadness. He sat down and began to talk to her, reliving all of their adventures the year before from their initial meeting at the café to Jerusalem discussing all they had shared.

Lyle told her she would always be in his heart and would miss her. He prayed and thanked God that she had come into his life, even for a short time. Friends are hard to find. Leuviah, you did something guardian angels are not supposed to do. You brought Eva's spirit there. She arrived with a great smile seeing him, wrapped her arms around him, and whispered to him, "You will always be my friend. I love you and will be with you always." For just that moment, Lyle smiled, feeling her warm embrace surround him. He smiled and said, "Eva, I love you." He turned away, never to visit the grave again. Leuviah, I thank you for caring so much for Lyle and doing this. God appreciates it too. I know Lyle spent the remainder of the transit to the Gulf reading her letters, laughing and reliving all she had conveyed to him. This brightened up his days until he could truly put the sadness away. One solace during this sad period was letters from his wife and kids sharing stories about their days. Leuviah, I was wrong, some humans (men and women) can have a loving friendship. God is good.

I fear more sadness is to follow.

Briathos

Stoic Leuviah,

It is good to see Lyle is spending time with the staff chaplain seeking guidance in his spiritual well-being. He is attending the ship's Sunday services. The chaplain is helping Lyle through his pain and sadness while dealing with Eva's death. The sessions are reaping results and putting Lyle's sprite on an even plain. I know one of the most difficult challenges for all of the men on ships during extended cruises is loneliness. Being away from their families for extended periods of time can be so painful. Missing family events or helping to solve life's problems are most challenging. We have seen the results when they go ashore for respite. Many go directly to the local bars, drink heavily, and fornicate with the local prostitutes. Guilt and loneliness drives many to these behaviors. Guardian angels must be ever so diligent protecting these men when most vulnerable. On the last port visit, I noticed Lyle did go to the local bar. He had some drinks with local bar girls. You could see the enemy encouraging him to drink more and telling him how nice it would be to lay with the woman he was talking. Well, thanks to you and your efforts, he refrained from participating in those behaviors. Of all your reports the main office has received, this was one of the most disconcerting evil events since you were assigned to protect this soul. Three days after entering the Central Gulf, the patrols were being monitored by the staff, ensuring all ship escorts were following orders. One protocol required is known as DE-confliction. The two belligerents fly air attacks over the Gulf as their primary thoroughfare. All neutral ships needed a method for communicating to the aircraft. Radio operators transmit to the belligerent aircraft, communications identifying the ship as neutral and to stay outside the ship's missile firing range. For the past two years, this protocol worked perfectly, protecting both the ship and belligerent aircraft. It was almost time for the group to transit home. The replacement commander was transiting the Arabian Sea, en route to the Gulf via the straits. The commander had been warned the belligerent country to the east may be positioning their ships to harass or attack and block the shipping lanes. The admiral had ordered Lyle to travel via helio to the Arabian Sea and meet with the new commander. The purpose was to brief the commander on possible hostilities. Upon arriving, he briefed the commander on all current activities in the area. The day after arriving, the ship began its transit through the straits. Around midday, the radio operator picked up belligerent aircraft twenty miles away, flying from the south, heading in the general direction of the ship. The ship's company was already at battle station as standard procedure when transiting a war zone. Leuviah, you had already known something was happening. Guardian angels had warned you the belligerent country's pilots had been ordered to fly directly toward the ship as it moved through the straits. Your counterparts were worried about what their charges were going to do. The guardian angels were working diligently to persuade the pilots not to engage the ship. About 1:00 pm, the ship's radio operator began warning the aircraft, stating, "This a neutral war ship transiting international waters. You must change course. If you come within one mile, you will be fired upon." The ship was transmitting over clear channels that all aircraft military and civilian monitor. There would be no reason the aircraft would fail to respond. Tensions in the ship's combat center were high. The danger—this was the ship's first communications engagement, a new inexperienced crew and a commander who ran his ship as a Captain Queeg. You knew this could end in disaster. You saw a demon ratcheting up the tension, whispering in the commander's ear, "Shoot the aircraft down. They are getting close and would kill your ship and its crew." The demon whispered to the commander, "What about your wife and kids? If you do not fire now, you may be killed. Your poor family will be all alone." As the aircraft closed within three miles, the radio operator yelled, "Sir, there are two aircraft inbound." Panic was noticeable on the crew and commander's faces. The commander ordered the weapons officer to get missiles on the rail in preparation to be fired. Demons were dancing everywhere, sensing the anxiety and tension, hoping that many souls would be devoured this day. Guardian angels busied themselves providing as much soothing calm as the humans would listen to. It was a difficult challenge. Once chaos begins, it is difficult to get under control. The radio operator was doing all he could to encourage the aircraft to change course to no avail. When the aircraft came within two miles, the commander ordered the fire control team to direct the fire control radar on the aircraft. This fire control radar would be picked up by the aircraft. This was a warning that the ship's next step would be to fire missiles to protect itself. The tension could be physically felt throughout the ship, not only by the crew but by all spiritual beings. The radio operator screamed, "Sir, the aircraft are closing directly on us; they are within the one mile down range." The ship's weapons officer ran to the radar, confirming the aircraft were still closing. Lyle spoke to the commander, telling him, "Sir, based on my experience, this is usual behavior for the belligerent's pilots. Sir, be patient. They will change course shortly." The radar operator informed the commander he thought something was strange. He was reading two military aircraft flying at them. He also could see what he thought was third aircraft. The commanding officer ask if he were certain.

The response was an infatic NO! Military aircraft broadcast a radar signature that identifies them as military aircraft. Time was moving quickly. The commander had to make a decision for the safety of his crew. Shoot or not to shoot? His mind was spinning, and the demon was in his head, yelling, "SHOOT, SHOOT!" The radar operator reported the aircraft were within one-half of a mile and closing. The radio operator was doing his best to communicate to the aircraft directing them to change course. Lyle began to pray, asking for protection of the ship and that the aircraft would change course. The commander said, "Missiles released authorized." The entire Combat Center became so quiet that one could hear a pin drop. Just seconds before the missiles left the ship, a forward lookout panicking with excitement reported, "I see a civilian aircraft heading toward us about a quarter of a mile out. OH! My God, that is the same direction as the military aircraft." The lookout continued, "I see two jet fighters peeling off from under the civilian aircraft, leaving the area." The commander was dumbstruck. There was a familiar "swoosh" sound, indicating two missiles had just been released to a target. Now, two of his missiles were heading directly at a civilian aircraft, and he could not stop it. The radio operator attempted to warn the civilian aircraft, screaming into the radio, "Unknown aircraft, we have just fired two missiles in your direction, take any evasive action as you can!" The effort was for naught. Suddenly, there was a massive explosion. The sky lit up with a great fireball. Everyone in the Combat Center knew their missiles had struck the civilian aircraft. The horror felt was one of stunned silence. Lyle grabbed a radio and began to report to his boss what had just transpired. The ship's lookout and bridge crew saw the impact and watched with horror as the civilian plane began to break up and fall in pieces out of the sky. Most disturbing was the bodies flying out everywhere. Everyone on the ship knew there would be no survivors. The plane and parts crashed into the water. Nothing but plane parts and bodies could be seen EVERYWHERE in the water. All the angels in the area could be seen hovering over those who had died. They lifted the souls up and took them to heaven. You could see a struggle between some of the guardian angels and demons over a soul or two. In some cases, it was not clear which direction a soul should be taken. Remember, upon a human's death, when there is a question whether the soul qualifies for heaven, angels error on the side of the Father and take them up for judgment. You reported never seeing such evil and despair on display that day. The demons were dancing on the water with exuberance, excited with their success in bring down the civilian aircraft. Demons grabbed their victims, tearing limbs and arms as they descended to hell. Their master's hope was as a result of this incident, other countries would enter the conflict; more souls to consume in hell. Hell on earth would be experienced by Lyle and the crew this day. The ship sent recovery boats into the water to pick up the bodies. Lyle offered to assist in the gruesome task. There were women, children, and old folks alike who needed to be recovered. In some cases, there were only parts to pick up. It took many boats two days to collect the 120 bodies. The commander and his crew were so confused as to what had happened. The incident investigation determined the belligerent county's military aircraft put the civilian aircraft a risk. The fighters intentionally flew and remained under the civilian aircraft's wings until the ship's missiles were fired. This was seen and reported by the lookout. This deception caused confusion for radar operators. In that the military aircraft transmit a specific radio frequency, the civilian aircraft could not be mistaken as military. It was an evil ruse perpetrated by the belligerent country at the expense of its citizens. When Lyle arrived back on the flag ship, the admiral gave him a few days off to work through the anxiety and sadness experienced. You have some work to do. Lyle may have some emotional challenges coming to grips with this ugly, evil tragedy. Stay close. Remember how he lost his way when his father died.

Your brother in Christ,
Briathos

Leuviah, grace and peace be with you.

I see Lyle's group made it back home only to find out as they left the ship, they were getting underway the next day and taking another group of ships to the North Atlantic for training. It was wonderful of you to speak with his wife and children's guardian angels, discussing what they could do to ease the pain, missing him so much. He had been gone for six months and now was leaving again; no time for the family. It did concern me. I received a report his wife was not doing well with the extended separations. She was emotionally weak, someone needing direction and support in her life. This could become a problem. The demons were whispering in her ear, "Resent him for being gone. You need love and attention he is not providing. Maybe you should find a substitute in his absence." Hahaiah, her guardian angel, has his work cut out. I have seen many of these long-term relationships go sideways, resulting in divorce. Lyle has a big heart and compassion for others. Consider when they were underway traveling far up in the North Atlantic. He had befriended a young sailor (John) who was on his first cruse. At nineteen, this was the first time away from home. John grew up in a little town called Flat Rock in the mountains of West Virginia. He missed his family and especially his girlfriend, Malinda. They planned to marry after he returned from the cruise. John had been dating his girlfriend, Malinda, since seventh grade. He frequently said he knew someday he would marry her. The North Atlantic is a dangerous place at sea in the winter. John's guardian angel Cahetel discussed her concerns with you about the young sailor's well-being. John had been receiving letters from Malinda, discussing how much she needed him. She wrote she did not know how much longer she could wait; she needed a man. This disturbed him greatly. Cahetel was doing all he could to bolster John's emotional state. He visited John in dreams, showing him how wonderful Malinda was. One vision in his memory showed the day Malinda told him she would wait for him; she loved him. Lyle spent time with John, encouraging him to keep writing positive letters to her. He should remind her how happy they would be when they were together again. The demons were working overtime to impress upon John that doom was at hand, encouraging him to despise her for feeling the way she did. It was her fault. Cahetel reported that she was losing the battle and concerned that if John received another ugly letter, it may go bad for him. Lyle encouraged John to pray to God for help in relieving his anxiety and protection for Malinda. The ship pulled into the Scottish port for a short rest. Lyle did an outstanding job giving John emotional support, distracting him from his sadness. They took in the local sights, eating dinner at the same restaurant every afternoon. The distraction appeared to lift John's spirits. They sat at the same table for each meal, served by the same waitress. Lyle and the waitress enjoyed joking with each other while she served them. During the four days in port, he and the John got to know their waitress. She told them her name was Ailsa and had lived in the area her entire life. Interestingly, her name means "consecrated to God." They discussed families, friends, and life's desires. It was a great distraction from being at sea on the dark gray desolate water. On the last day, Ailsa encouraged them to be sure to visit her when they returned. Just before getting underway, two months of mail was delivered to the ship. As the ship got underway, there was great excitement in anticipation of getting news from home. The ship left port and ran into a great storm. The sea height was between thirty and forty-foot high waves. As the ship rolled from side to side, sometimes leaning forty-eight degrees to one side or the other. Sailors were lifted off of their beds onto the wall. As the ship righted itself, the men fell back onto the bed. Lyle had never been in a storm like this. As the ship rolled from one side, it would shudder as it moved. Many of the crew were sick. The second day out, Lyle went looking for his friend John to see if he had received any mail from home. He found him in his bed, crying. When ask what was wrong, he handed Lyle a letter. As he read the letter, he learned that John's girlfriend told him she could not live in a relationship as theirs anymore. The separation was too difficult to handle and was now dating someone else. She said she was sorry and would always love him but could not be separated for so long. He was devastated. Lyle and Chaetel (sailor's guardian angel) did all they could to keep his spirits up. John kept reading the letter on and off for the next two days. Demons were working on him, telling him, "You have nothing to live for; give up on life." Chaetel did all she could to balance the sadness he was feeling. She felt she was losing him. I see Lyle spent many hours with John keeping his spirits up. One day during a storm, Lyle went looking for John to have lunch. As he was walking down the passageway, he saw John walking in the opposite direction with a life jacket on. He was heading to the a port side exit hatch. The weather was so bad that all crew were restricted from going on deck. Lyle became alarmed; his heart was racing, realizing what might be happening. He ran toward John, yelling, "STOP! Don't go out there!" John looked at Lyle, smiled, opened the hatch, and exited. Lyle got to the exit hatch quickly, went out, and saw John leaning on the safety lines. The stormy ocean sea waves were crashing all around, and it was difficult to see him. Cold, dark gray waves made it difficult for Lyle to remain standing. The angry sea crashed violently against the ship, pitching and rolling. Lyle was afraid he may be washed into the sea at any time. Holding onto the lifeline, waves crashing upon him, he was yelling, "John! Come back in! It's not that bad!" Suddenly, John looked at Lyle and took off the life vest. As he straddled the rail, he yelled, "Without her, I have nothing worth living for." Leuviah, you could see the demons with great excitement turn toward you with that evil sneer, encouraging him to jump, telling him, "Your life is over. Without your Malinda, you are nothing." He leaned over the side, looked at Lyle, and smiled as he was swept away by the angry sea. Lyle saw him for just a second before he disappeared into an angry wave. Lyle yelled, "Man overboard!" The ship's alarms were initiated. Sailors are trained to not take their eyes off someone who has fallen overboard. Once eyes are averted, they lose sight of the person. The person is swallowed up and never seen again. Although he did not move his eyes from John, in what seemed like seconds, he was consumed by the angry waves. John was gone so fast that it seemed like a dream to Lyle. The chance he would survive the jump was nil. You did see the demons holding John's soul by its ankle, looking at you and Chaetel, smiling, and yelling, "I got one!" It was a sad day for guardian angels and Lyle. Lyle's first emotion was anger that this young man would take his life because of someone's selfishness. He slowly moved from the rail and back inside. Soaked from head to toe, he was taken to medical for a checkup and sent to his bed to recover. Anguish consumed Lyle as he relived the events of that day, trying to make some sense of what happened. Stay close to Lyle. He will need your angelic love and strength.

You are in God's grace.
Briathos

Leuviah, my friend,

Your most recent report is fraught with despair, emotional growth, and some positive hope. Lyle is very distraught after witnessing his friend's suicide. He is so angry and confused, wondering how this could happen and consumed with the question, "How can one selfish person's lack of loyalty and self-control contribute to destroying another person's life?" Leuviah, you did a good job suggesting he discuss his feelings with the ship's chaplain, reminding him that through prayer and the power of God, he can find solace and understanding. It appeared to lighten his load. The disconcerting part is his anger toward God, thinking, "Why did God not protect John and keep him from killing himself and damning his young soul to hell?" Lyle believes a person who commits suicide will be damned to hell. I know the demons had infiltrated John's mind with guilt, telling him, "It is your fault John killed himself." As his anger and despair grew, so did the power and excitement for the enemy. That is the thing about free will; we do all we can to positively influence the humans, but in the end, it is their choice. The main office has sent Chaetel for a rest. She was so saddened with her inability to keep John from the clutches of evil that she doubted her ability to help other souls. After some respite, she will recover and be reassigned. I see your ward is making some progress and was excited to see the ship pull into Scotland for one week of rest. He planned to go to John and his favorite café and hopefully see Ailsa. You know how he enjoyed visiting the local sights and eating food. The second day in, he made it to the café and sat at John and his favorite table. He was in awe, sitting in the café looking out over the cliffs and bay with the beautiful blue sky and the weather warm and calm. It brought him some peace. While daydreaming, he heard a familiar voice calling out his name with great joy and excitement. Ailsa asked where his friend was. With tears welling up in his eyes, he described his friend's death. She began to cry, expressing her sincere sorrow for the loss. He asked her to sit while he ordered. They reminisced about he and John's fun they had during the last port visit. Leuviah, I know you saw all the signs that this might be a problem. Here was Lyle, sad for the loss, coupled with the many months being away from his family. This had all the makings of trouble. Here was a tall, beautiful, woman with dark hair and stark blue eyes consoling him. Before he left, she told him to come and visit her at her apartment if he needed someone to talk to about this sad incident. Well, he did take her up on the offer. For the next four days, Ailsa and Lyle spent all day and late into the evening together enjoying the local sights, food, and each other's company. Based on your observations, this was going to be another Israel incident with no real sinning impact. It is interesting that he stayed at her apartment for the remainder of his visit, sleeping in the spare room. I know demons were coaxing him, causing him to think how much he cared for this woman and whether he loved her. On the last night in town, they went to a local community social event, enjoying each other's company immensely. At a one point that evening, they were dancing a slow dance. Holding her close, he could smell her hair, perfume, and felt her soft, supple body. Closing his eyes, he felt he wanted to be nowhere else. When humans are emotionally compromised because of trauma or sadness, they have a tendency to gravitate to anyone who can provide respite from the agony. Ailsa was that conduit. The enemy was working overtime. Demons softly spoke, "Lyle, she is so beautiful, soft, tender, and her perfume is intoxicating. Take her tonight. No one will know." This amplified those feelings he was having. Demons were projecting images to him, seeing himself lying in here bed, holding her naked, warm body in his. It was stirring primal urges he had not expected. While dancing, she looked up at him with those beautiful blue eyes and kissed him. She told him she was falling in love with him. This was a shock to him. He stopped for a moment, hugged her, then walked her off of the dance floor. His head was spinning. You reminded him of his family and how important loyalty was. Demons screamed, "Take her. She is yours. Be damned the consequences. No one would know." He took her hand, saying it was time they went back to her apartment. Thoughts swam in his; could he do this? Be with this woman for the night? Of course, he was being egged on by the demons. A great struggle was running through his head all the way back to her apartment. Demons screamed, "You care for her." Leuviah countered, "God loves you, and this is not his way." When they arrived at the door, he stopped before opening it. He turned to her and told her he was having unexplained feelings for her and truly cared for her, but his conscious would not allow him to pursue spending the night in her bed. He loved his family and would not do anything to destroy that. They walked inside. Ailsa went straight to her bedroom. Throughout the night, Lyle could hear her weeping. The next morning, both woke and made breakfast without a word being said. As Lyle packed up his belongings, he said, "I need to get back. We are leaving late tonight." As he walked to the door, he turned to Ailsa and handed her a piece of paper with the ship's address. Lyle asked, "Could you write me? I would like to know how you are doing." Ailsa grabbed the paper with tears in her eyes, ran to him, and hugged him passionately, whispering, "I did fall in love with you. I understand why you cannot love me."

She ran to her room crying. Lyle walked out and jumped into a cab. While traveling, he realized how sad he was, wondering why he did not see what was happening before it did. His last thought was, "I will never see her again, and I hope she will find someone." On the drive back, Lyle prayed for forgiveness for what he had thought of doing. As you know, he has three primary loyalties he lives by: love of God, love of country, and love of family. Loyalty is his way of life. This enabled you to keep him from falling into the demon-driven passion. I see it was nip and tuck. Wow, you are earning your wings. Keeping this ward on the straight and narrow is a monumental task. I fear this is not the last you will see of Ailsa. Once humans find what they believe is love, they can be driven to do unusual things. Consider Lyle's young friend John, who lost his love and was driven to suicide. I know the demons had their part in the unfortunate incident.

Be watchful and on guard.

Briathos

Dearest Leuviah,

Wow! I thought the Scottish woman incident was behind you and Lyle once they departed Scotland. Humans are amazing beings. Once they feel they are in love, it seems no amount of time and space can keep the person from searching for that love. The way I understand it, after leaving Scotland, Lyle's ship conducted exercises in the North Atlantic Ocean. Nice to the see no major problems occurred during that time. He was still grappling with his friend John's suicide and also thinking of Ailsa and how she comforted him with his sadness. Lyle continued to pray for guidance and relief from that sadness. The ship pulled into Portsmouth, England, over 500 miles from Scotland. Once the ship was anchored, Lyle disembarked to visit local sights. As he stepped off the gangway, he saw Ailsa running toward him with a huge smile, calling out his name. I could see your surprise matched Lyle's. She jumped into his arms and with great passion embraced him. They went to the local café to talk and catch up. Ailsa told him that she knew he loved her as a friend, but she wanted more. Lyle replied, "I love one woman, my wife." The demons were urging her to entice him, whispering, "You want him. Get back to your hotel room." The demons continued, "If you can only get him to your room, you will win his love. He is vulnerable and weak, and you can win his love." Aniel (Ailsa's guardian angel) battling the demons, charged into Ailsa's mind, saying, "You know he is married and cannot be with you. Trust in God's love and guidance and do what is right. If you truly love him, you must not pursue this evil act." Leuviah, you did well, reminding Lyle of his family and that God would not approve of this sin. The seven deadly sins are difficult to overcome in a human's mind, a challenge to face when a soul ascends to heaven and faces judgment. As the enemy knows, they can use guilt on those who commit sins, causing humans to spiral down deeper into evil ways. Because of your diligence, he did not put himself in a position to weaken his resolve. He saw her beauty and wonderful personality. This, coupled with the long separation from his wife, he knew how difficult it was to be near her. Loneliness is the most dangerous feeling a human can experience. Consider in the past three years, he has been home with his family a total of 1.5 months. Not continuous! Humans need companionship, someone to go to in times is stress. He had no one. They spent the next two days together. Meeting at the café each morning. He convinced her to return home. They parted as friends. Lyle paid for her transportation home. They said their goodbyes, knowing they would never see one another again. I believe they were truly good friends, and each had become better humans. They did exchange addresses, promising to write. The efforts you made, reminding him he would soon be home with his family, brightened his spirit. You could see the demons' rage as they saw his joy. The enemy hates humans, especially those who are joyful. I received word from Hahaiah (his wife's guardian angel) that trouble was amiss. The demons were weaving their charms negatively, influencing her moral decisions. You see his friend who was supposed to be on this four-month cruise stayed behind due to a serious oral, dental infection. It required eliminating the infection, then oral surgery. Being a good friend, before leaving, he discussed with his wife whether his friend could stay at the house until the serious problem was resolved. This is what friends do. Lyle and his family were generous and would help anyone needing assistance. Trouble was brewing, and I hope Hahaiah is able to infuse

God's spirit into this lonely, weak woman. Stay on guard. I fear a storm is coming!

Briathos

My loving brother Briathos,

As you predicted, THE STORM ARRIVED! This is an event that may crush Lyle's soul.

One hundred twenty days after leaving, the ship pulled back into the home port. The excitement on the ship was overwhelming. Everyone discussed what they were going to do first once they had reunited with their family. An interesting thing about human beings on a ship that has been gone for so long: there is a loneliness felt by each man that cannot be quenched by other sailors around them. They fill their days with work to dull the pain, best known as being alone in a crowd. So coming home to family is an auspicious occasion. After Lyle left the ship, he saw his wife waiting in the car. He ran to the car, noticing the children were not there. She does not get out of the car to greet him. She rolled down the window and said in a dower voice, "Hi. Let's go home." Lyle entered the passenger side and reached out to hug and kiss her. She pulled away and pushed him back. He looked with confusion and asked, "What is wrong? Why are the children not with you?" She turned, looked him straight in the eye, and told him, "I no longer want to be a mother or wife. I want to be free of all responsibility and do what I want; this life has destroyed me as a person." He was stunned. In a confused state, he asked, "What's wrong, and why are you doing this?" After being away for so long, he was dumbfounded. There was nothing in her letters that indicated her anxiety and desire to be "free." He could not wrap his head around what she had said and why. She put the vehicle in drive and headed home. You could have heard a pin drop the entire trip home. Lyle was contemplating in his mind, trying to figure out what may have driven her to this. When he was home, they had fun together and worked with the kids, helping them to grow as people, never fighting or arguing about anything. They arrived home, she handed him separation documents, and said, "I moved into a hotel on the beach." He asked, "Isn't there anything we can do to fix this? Could we go to counseling to figure out the problem?" She yelled, "I DO NOT WANT TO BE A WIFE OR MOTHER! You can have the kids." Birathos, with all the love the Father gives, I did not think it was possible for a heart to be so sad. I consoled him with kind words, reminding him God was with him, even more so during times of strife. It did not work. Pain was oozing from him. Anger would be the next emotion I knew I would see. Brother, I prayed the Father would ease his pain. When he left the ship, walking to the car, I knew something was happening. Demons were everywhere in the vehicle, cheering their comrade who was poisoning the wife's mind. They were laughing at me, saying, "We have this soul (wife). She committed adultery in his absence." To further cause him pain, he had to tell the children their parents were separated and would be getting divorced. The children sobbed. The girls were fourteen and twelve years old. This was devastating to them. There had never been any indication of problems. Their parents did everything together and supported them in all of their extracurricular activities. I felt the heavy weight of depression in the household. One night Lyle had called his father-in-law to get some advice. Lyle informed him what was happening and all the sad details. Suddenly, the father-in-law, starting yelling, "SHE IS SLEEPING WITH SOMEONE! THAT IS THE ONLY REASON SHE WANTS TO END THE MARRAGE WITHOUT TRYING TO FIX IT!" I saw demons standing next to Lyle, whispering, "That is what she must have done," telling him, "You should track the person down and KILL them both!" I could see the rage building in his eyes as he realized that was what she had done. Birathos, as you remember, loyalty is one of the basic tenants he lives by. To break this would be more than a sin in his eyes; destruction is the answer to relieve the pain. After all, they had been married almost sixteen years. He would tell strangers and friends alike how wonderful their relationship was. He felt so happy and at peace with the relationship, and he compared it to that old pair of tennis shoes you had that fit so well that they could never be given away. Instead of helping, the father-in-law's call infuriated Lyle more. Demons continued to stoke his anger, hoping he would act on it and take a human life. I became more concerned when in his past prayers, he would ask God why he would torment him with this pain. That was the last prayer he said. Demons poisoned Lyle's mind, telling him, "This is God's fault." Two days later, he hired a private investigator to see what his wife had been up to. He was walking in a fog cloud while putting on a positive face for his children. He could barely function. One evening, their old friends were having a party at their house in the country. During the party, one of his wife's friends had drank mass quantities of alcohol and was not focused. While talking to him, she let it slip that she knew his wife was having an affair with his best friend who had stayed at his house. A demon had been standing next to the woman and pushed her to share with Lyle the information she had. This further compounded his anger and sadness. Not only did his wife of fifteen years committed adultery, but it was also with his best friend. Birathos, how could this be any worse? The remainder of the evening, he drank excessively. It is not in his character to do this. I did all I could to convince him to stop drinking. His sadness and anger were overwhelming. The demons were winning the day. The more he drank, the angrier he got. Finally, he jumped into his jeep to leave. His friends tried to stop him but failed. The demons were jumping with glee, telling Lyle to drive and drive as fast as he could. This would relieve the pain. He was exceeding seventy miles per hour down country roads; with the exception of his headlights, no other illumination was around. The demons were telling him to go faster. I did all I could to influence him to slow down, stop, and sleep off the alcohol. His rage was so great that there was no stopping him. Suddenly, his eye became heavy, and he was going to pass out. I kept pressing him. The demons were screaming, "Faster, faster," waiting for him to drive off the road, crash, and die. He passed out, and the jeep swerved to the right. My wings were wrapped around him, telling him I would protect him. The road was three feet above a cornfield. When the jeep left the road, it flew five feet into the air, with the wind in his face and the jeep top down. With the exception of the headlights, night was all-encompassing. I was afraid this would end his life. The jeep pitched and dipped slightly, causing the front end to strike the ground first. For one second, the jeep was suspended with the front end burred in the ground. Wobbling back and forth, I was not sure if it would fall forward, crushing Lyle, or back on its tires. I was pulling the jeep back to get it to land on the tires. I looked in front of me, and the enemy had been pulling the jeep forward in hopes of it landing on its top so Lyle would be crushed and killed. Demons yelled, "Give up. We will kill your charge this night!" The jeep fell back onto the tires and settled there. Lyle awoke, unaware of what had happened. He looked around in the blackness, realizing he had driven off the road and was in a cornfield. He decided to sleep there until daylight, knowing he would be sober and able to figure out where he was. Brother, I have never seen the demons so enraged about losing a charge. They were screaming, whining, and pounding the ground. They thought this was the night Lyle would die. They were going to attempt to take his soul, even though he was in the Father's grace. I told them as much. That only outraged them even more. The next morning, with the sun blazing in his eyes, he got out of the jeep to assess the damages. He was amazed to see, with the exception of a few scratches, that the jeep was in good order. He realized he had been going too fast, left the road, jumped the ditch, and landed in a cornfield. I guess because I had protected him, he was unharmed. Keeping the jeep from landing on its top and possibly killing Lyle broke the interference rules. We can protect charges with our wings and through whispers to the mind but should not influence the outcome as in this case. I know I am not to meddle and should allow free will to win the day. Wasn't there enough suffering? The love of his life was leaving, and he was going to be responsible for raising two teenage girls on his own. His career required him to transfer frequently throughout the world. My love for this ward is strong. I did not want the worst moment in his life to be his last. I will take any discipline you, the main office, or the Father has for me. I see great things in the human, given time. He has a good heart. I have been assigned to protect him and will do so to my utmost ability.

Your servant in Christ,
Leuviah

My gallant sister Leuviah,

After reading your letter and explanation on what you did to help Lyle, I have had discussions with the main office. The leaders were satisfied with your explanation on the events. In fact, they send their love and appreciation. Guardian angels are the loving link between the Father and humans. Most carry the charges' prayers to the Father as their advocate. The report I received yesterday caused much pain to hear. We are losing Lyle to the darkness. I see he has been drinking alcohol often. I am certain this is directly related to his family situation. So as I see in the report, one evening, a few weeks after the jeep incident, he was sitting at the dining room table drinking excessively. He had just reviewed a report provided by a private investigator he hired. It confirmed his wife was sleeping with his best friend. The report provided the address and location of the hotel they were staying in. It also included obscene photos of the two together. The demons were in his head, pushing him. "Drink more; the pain will go away." Ideas were flowing from the demons, telling him, "They are sick and disloyal. How can a wife of fifteen years and a best friend do this to you? Someone has to end these people. They must pay for the heinous acts they have been doing!" Demons told him, "These people have no honor and should be scratched from the earth. They are destroying your children's lives because of lust. They should be killed!" All at once, Lyle jumped up and went into a closet in his bedroom and extracted a shotgun. He returned to the dining room and began loading it, muttering, "Those disloyal pukes—they need to die and feel the pain they have inflected on me and the kids." As he loaded the shotgun, his fourteen-year-old daughter came down the stairs and walked into the kitchen. There she saw the empty whiskey bottle and Lyle loading the shotgun. She was afraid, asking him, "Dad, what are you doing with the gun?" He abruptly got up without a word and headed for the garage. She ran after him, not knowing where he was going or what he was going to do. I know you were warding off the demons, telling him, "This was not God's way. It is God who will judge their sins, not humans." Lyle was not listening. He jumped into the jeep and headed for the addresses given to him by the private investigator. Lyle's primary thought was that they would feel his pain and send them to hell! I know you were afraid when he said, "THEY WILL DIE." You lovingly spoke to him, saying, "Killing is a sin." In a calm, steady voice, he said, "I know killing is wrong, but in this case, I am willing to pay the price on judgment day." You were losing him. I see you did have some help trying to avoid this mess. Seheiah (the daughter's guardian angel) was attempting to calm her and whispered, "Call a family friend for help." As the daughter sat on the floor with the garage door open, she decided to call her father's Navy friend to see what he could do. She ran to the phone and dialed the number. When the friend answered, she was yelling, "Help my dad! He just left with his loaded shotgun. I saw a report that proved Mom was sleeping with Dad's friend who had been staying at the house. He has been drinking. Dad said as he was leaving, 'I am going to take care of those disloyal pukes tonight!' Please stop him." Lyle headed for the beach motel, knowing that whoever answered the door would be the first person killed. Between the demons' antagonism and the alcohol, his rage was almost out of control. He got off the freeway and was driving on the beach. One block from the motel, he stopped at a red light. Suddenly, out of nowhere, a truck screeched to a halt in front of the jeep. Someone jumped out of the truck, calling Lyle's name. Lyle recognized the friend's voice. The friend walked up to the open jeep (the top was off) and began talking to him, asking him, "What are you doing at the beach? The girls are home alone." He asked, "Should you not be home with the girls?" Lyle responded, "I have a couple of things to take care of, then I will head home." The friend was looking around the jeep and saw the shotgun. He reached inside and grabbed the shotgun. He held it up and asked, "What are you planning to do with this?" The response was clear. "I have photos with the two of them together. They need to die for the pain they caused. Evil begets evil. I will be the reaper." The friend ejected all the shells out of the gun. He told Lyle, "I will keep it safe for you." Lyle was getting visibly angry, and demons screamed in his ear, pushing him to tell the friend to get out of his way. He had to clean up the mess. The friend suggested they go to the bar on the corner and talk about what he was planning to do. He said to Lyle, "If after a couple of beers and conversation, you still want to kill someone, I will not stand in your way." The friend told him. "I will put the shotgun in my trunk for safekeeping until we work things out. " Lyle appeared less angry and acquiesced. They both parked their vehicles and went into the bar. Although we do not condone alcohol consumption by our charges, this was an excellent way to divert Lyle from danger. I see as it turns out, the friend drove him safely home. No harm was done to his wife and the man she was with. Leuviah, I know this will cause you a great deal of work to get Lyle on the right path. He is in a dark place. If not for his children and dedication to his duty, I am afraid he will slip down that rabbit hole and never return.

You said you heard him ask as he fell asleep, "Why is God doing this to me? He hates me. I have no reason to pray for anything because no good comes from it. Look at the evil that has befallen me and especially my innocent daughters. Lord, I pray that evil pounces on my ex-wife and ex-best friend. Death is not good enough." Your stomach must have turned when you saw the evil smirks and twinkling in the demon's eyes. I know your resolve. You will help him overcome this evil.

When need is great, God's love is most.

Birathos

Leuviah;

It has been months since your last report. I see Lyle's disposition has not improved. He presents a positive demeanor around his children. It has devastated him. Because of his own parents' breakup, Lyle dreamed of having a wife and children to care for. For the first fifteen years, it was so. Something changed in his wife. It is as if she was possessed and driven to evil. I do know that while he was away, demons were taking advantage of her loneliness, pushing her to get close to his friend. Once on that side, she could not find her way back. To compound his depressed state, he had orders to transfer. Lyle's youngest daughter asked to move with him. Two months ago, I see he transferred to a new job in the city near where he grew up. In his state, he renewed friendships with old criminal friends. Why was he associating with old friends he knew from the camp days? Most had been killed or jailed at one time. Evil exuded from these people; drugs and crime-ridden souls looking for more to join their ranks. He continued to do well at work and had taken a young man (Andrea) under his guidance. Andrea had grown up in the city and was trying to break away from his old associates. His old friends were hardened criminals dealing drugs and committing untold crimes. Andrea is a weak soul and is bent to the will of the demons and coaxed by his friends. After many discussions and guidance from Lyle, Andrea decided it was time to move away from his former friends. Two days after the conversation with Lyle, Andrea told his friends to stay away from him and his baby, saying, "I want nothing to do with you guys." One day he informed Lyle that his old friends had been busted for narcotics and he was accused of reporting them to the local police. He said they had threatened to kill him for being a snitch. Two days later, Lyle received a panicked call from the Andrea, screaming, "They are after me! Help!" He told Andrea, "Drive to your house, get inside, and lock the door. I will meet you there. Stay on the phone with me until I get there." Lyle put Andrea on hold and called the police, reporting the threat. The police said since there was no crime being committed or credible threat, there was nothing they could. Lyle drove as fast as possible to get to the house. When he arrived, he saw Andrea's car in the drive. He was still sitting in it. Lyle got out of his car and began walking toward Andrea's car. Leuviah, I know you could see the demons standing on the car, jumping up and down with glee! They were almost ravenous with excitement. Something evil was going to happen. Andrea's guardian angel was standing outside of the car, looking on with anguish on her face and tears running down. She calmly shouted to you, "Andrea's name is not listed in the Book of Life. It time for his soul to be lifted up. I will not be escorting him to heaven. His soul is lost! I have failed my assignment." You got closer to Lyle and whispered, "Be careful. Something is wrong." As Lyle got near the car, you saw danger closing in. Three men with automatic weapons jumped out of a nearby parked car. Suddenly, gunfire erupted everywhere. With bullets flying into the car, you wrapped your wings around Lyle, urging him to run and jump behind a parked car to his left. You both watched in horror as the three men stood and fired hundreds of bullets into the car. Andrea's guardian angel stood wailing in sadness and pain as death closed in. The smell of gunpowder was overwhelming. The sound of bullets hitting the with a "ting" sound would be with Lyle for a long time. The assailants were screaming. Lyle could hear Andrea screaming in pain. "MY BABY! SAVE MY BABY!" The shooters were in a hurry to leave, not concerned with Lyle. They ran to their car and drove away, car tires screeching. Lyle jumped up and ran to the car. Somehow Andrea was still alive. Blood was oozing out from everywhere. He could barely speak. There was blood spattered on the windows and dashboard. He sat slumped over the car and was mumbling, "My baby. How is my baby?" As he died, you did see the demons fighting over his soul, tearing at his legs. Each had a leg and was pulling as if it were a wishbone. The poor soul was screaming in fear and agony. Andreia's soul looked at you, pleading, "Don't let them take me to hell! Take care of my baby!" Unfortunately, it was only the beginning of terror for the soul. The vehicle was riddled with bullet holes. There must have been 100 to 200 holes. It looked like Swiss cheese. As Lyle stood there sickened and angry at the carnage, he heard crying. He looked in the back seat. There was a baby about five months old in a car seat. Lyle, yelled, "OH MY GOD, a baby." He ran to the back door, opened it, and pulled the baby out. By some miracle, she did not have a scratch. He screamed in amazement, "This is a miracle." It was then you saw Poyel (the little girl's guardian angel). Her broad smile lit up the sky. You said with a bright smile, "Poyel, it was you who saved the child." Poyel exclaimed, "That is my job. It was not her time. Many bullets flew at her, but none would strike." When the police arrived, they were amazed at the damage; so many holes, and not one struck the child in the back seat where the gun fire came from. The police said, "It is a miracle the child was not struck. No one should have survived this shooting." The police counted over 250 bullet holes in the vehicle. What irritated me the most in your report was the description of the demons you saw peering around a tree, sneering, and snickering, and yelling, "You cannot take them all the heaven." Leuviah, this incident strengthened Lyle's resolve that God was not around to help. His thoughts were,

"How could God let this young man with a child be killed?" You need to remind him that the Father has given humans free will. It was Andrea's choice to link himself to this evil. It was the criminals' choice to shoot and kill Andrea. Sadness overcame you as these killers' guardian angels spoke to you, saying, "These killers have cemented their special place in hell. We will not be able to protect them from their fate." Leuviah, God loves all his children but will not intervene when free will is in play. As you know, all human lives have an expiration date list in the Book of Life. This date can be accelerated when bad free will choices are made. In those cases, the life is shortened. This is done at their own peril. Visit Lyle in his dreams. Remind him of this and to be wise when making free will choices. My sister, be careful. Lyle is standing at a precipice and may fall deeper into the abyss. He is not attending church and has stopped praying. Until now, regardless of how his life was evolving, he always prayed. Now he has stopped. You must be ever so vigilant to get him back on the path.

Go with grace.

Briathos

Leuviah;

I see he is still associating with his old criminal friends. I would have thought that after Andrea's death, Lyle would cut off ties with his old friends. You reported he went to an illegal gun exchange. There were ten men from each side attending. A list of weapons included various handguns, shotguns, and AR 15s. During the negotiations, an argument broke out. Suddenly, guns were drawn, and a firefight ensued. Lyle was in a car waiting, not wanting to be involved. Bullets were flying everywhere, including hitting the car he was sitting in. You coaxed him out of the door and encouraged him to run for cover! As he ran for cover, you again protected him from being hit. He dove for cover behind a nearby building. You could see the fear and anxiety in his eyes. His heart was racing, and a thought occurred to him: "What the hell am I doing here? These are not my people!" It seems you have spent many years protecting this human, hoping he will see God's light. This may be the moment your efforts pay off and he does see the light and refrain from evil. He did have a gun, and once he was behind protection, for a twinkling of an eye, he raised the gun to fire. The dark place he has been in, coupled with the adrenaline flowing, was a perfect receipt for him to attack the shooters. The demon behind him was screaming, "KILL THEM THEY ARE FIRING AT YOU. You need to eliminate these evil beings from this earth." Nice job calming him and helping him to realize that to fire the gun would put him in a deep dark hole he may never come back from. He would become evil. The demons were raging mad, knowing they had lost an opportunity to drive Lyle further into darkness after committing this evil act. Demons wanted Lyle to kill someone, thus drawing him down into their evil soul-sucking realm. If Lyle had shot and killed someone, the demons could have used guilt to drive more hate and despair into Lyle's soul. These are incidents when many guardian angels lose their charge to the other side, never able to bring it back before death occurs. Those souls are taken to hell and devoured. Lyle saw his friend in trouble. A man was sneaking up behind his friend, preparing to fire. Just before the gun was fired, Lyle jumped from behind his cover and grabbed the man. They rolled around fighting for control of the gun. Lyle struck the man in the head, knocking him out. As he rose, a bullet hit him in the arm. He fell to the ground in pain. As he picked himself up and ran for cover, he saw his blood flowing everywhere. I saw your surprise, realizing you failed to protect him. Leuviah, considering the chaos, you did everything you could to protect him. This was his choice. Remember free will. His friends grabbed him from behind a building and directed him to a car to his right. They all jumped into the car and sped off. With wide eyes and visibly shaken, he mumbled, "I cannot believe I got involved in this." Lyle worried he would be caught and arrested, possibly put in jail. You sat there trying to calm him. I can imagine how crazed the demons were in the car, knowing how much chaos they caused that night but did not get a soul. They were not able to get Lyle killed or have him kill someone else. The demons had orders to ensure Lyle killed someone and was killed so they could take him to hell this night. Lyle was taken to a doctor for medical care; it was a doctor who performs illegal services for criminals. There would be no record of the care provided. The wound was a flesh wound; he would be ok. As he drove home that night, he realized how stupid he had been associating with the old criminal friends. He broke away from them many years ago and could not believe he jumped back into that life. That night, with great clarity, he resolved to end any relationship with these evil men. My dear sister, all of the work you have done over the years is paying off. With your guidance, after this scary encounter, he searched his soul and found he was better than how he was acting recently. Still angry about his family situation, he wanted to overcome the anger and sadness. This is God's love coming through you and helping Lyle see his value to God. Humans are difficult to figure out, free will and all. Leuviah, stay the course. Slowly you will win his soul back to God. He has returned to praying each night. Amen!

Briathos

Leuviah, my hard working sister,

I am glad to hear Lyle is healing well from the bullet wound. As I reflect on that night they shot him, it was you, Leuviah, who saved him from greater harm. You were not close enough to deflect the bullet that hit him. It was you calming him afterward and guiding him to safety. You are the shining light for Lyle. It is interesting to see how a crisis in one's life can have such an impact on these humans. Consider how he had fallen away from his spiritual life after being given divorce papers; blaming God, angry, and hating the world. Then the gang shooting incident caused him to pause and take stock to where he was going in his life. Fear has an interesting influence on humans. Sometimes they see the light and gravitate back to God, but others fall deeper into despair. It is the guardian angels who can make the difference on which direction is taken. I see you have been busy taking advantage of his reflection, reminding him that the road he was traveling on could only end in tragedy. Possibly, putting his soul in danger of being lost to Satan. I see he has begun praying, drinking less, and looking to associate with better friends. He remains skeptical around other humans after having the woman he loved and his best friend committing adultery. Lyle is unable to trust others. Helping him to trust and love may be your greatest challenge since your assignment began. I heard his prayers the other day and noticed he was praying for guidance to help overcome his anger and mistrust. When did he start wearing Buddhist meditation beads? I thought I heard him chanting. It appears he is searching for peace by exploring other religions again. That explains why you reported seeing a Buddhist guardian near Lyle during the shooting. Stay with him. This is a positive sign. He needs time to work through being lost and, with your guidance, find his way back to us. I am confident he will come back to us in the end. His Christian spirit is strong. How is it that Lyle gets himself into so many dangerous situations? You reported two months ago that while driving to work in the snow, he was feeling indestructible and driving too fast for the road conditions, thinking his jeep in four-wheel drive could go anywhere. You did remind him that he was inexperienced driving in winter weather. Fighting with the demons is always a challenge. The demons were pressing him, telling him, "You and the jeep are indestructible. Remember to experience the experience; be damned the consequences." He could barely see out of the windshield. Flying in the left lane of the highway and blowing past other vehicles, he did feel invincible. Suddenly, while going under a bridge, the jeep began to slide. He clutched the wheel and screamed, "OH GOD!" The jeep began to spin, traveling from the left lane in a clockwise circle. He knew there was nothing he could do, took his foot off of the gas, and released the steering wheel. Spinning rapidly, the jeep traveled into the center lane, then the right-hand lane. As the jeep hit the bridge side wall, it stood up on the right two wheels. You anticipated it would continue on that path and roll over. I know it was you, Leuviah, who stopped the momentum of the roll. Your efforts caused the jeep to continue spinning, moving back through the center lane, and stopping dead in the left lane where he started. As he sat there, shaken, thanked God for protection, restarted the jeep, and drove on to work. When he arrived at work, he told the story, finishing, saying this was most definitely a miracle. "How I missed hitting or being hit by other cars can only be explained by somebody looking after me." A friend said, "It must have been your guardian angel." Lyle laughed, thinking if that were the case, it explained how he had survived other dangerous incidents in his life. Leuviah, not only did I see you smile but felt its glow! There are those who know guardian angels look after assigned humans. You are a credit to all guardian angels.

Keep him safe.

Briathos

Leuviah, my old friend,

It has been three years since his divorce. I see you have been unsuccessful in helping to relieve his pain and distrust. His anger cannot seem to be relieved. You reported he has had visions tracking them down and destroying their lives. His biggest hurdle is the disloyalty from both the wife and his friend. He had thoughts "I should execute traitors." Leuviah, until he resolves this anger and hurt, he will not be able to move on. Know all of the main office is aware that demons are always in Lyle's ear, encouraging him to follow through on his vision. You have done well encouraging him to attend church services and become involved in the community. Expressing the desire for Lyle to find a companion and love is admirable. Be careful. Interference in human relationships is a dangerous thing. We know the Father made his children to be in pairs. He should not be alone. I see you are creatively working on helping Lyle. Aniel (the Scottish woman Ailsa's guardian angel) reported that he and you had a discussion about whether Ailsa still had thoughts and feelings for Lyle. The discussion included a suggestion for Aniel to visit Ailsa's dreams to revive images of Lyle and the pleasure she had in his company. Here I will summarize Aniel's efforts to determine Ailsa has fond memories and feelings for Lyle. One night as he entered her dreams, Ailsa saw Lyle sitting at a table in the café. He was looking in her direction, smiling, and waving to her to come over. She ran to him, and they embraced. Lyle whispered, "I have truly missed you and love you dearly." As the dream continued, the two of them walked into the fields, enjoying each other's company. Aniel observed as she lay in her bed, tears ran down her face, and she smiled beautifully.

Aniel knew these were tears of joy. Lyle and Ailsa walked and talked, holding hands, and discussing how wonderful it would be to spend the rest of their lives together. She awoke the next morning full of joy and sadness. She realized how much she cared for Lyle and wished her dream was a reality. Crying softly, she opened a drawer on the nightstand and pulled out a picture of her and Lyle. Reaching further into the drawer, she pulled out his last known mailing address. Aniel whispered softly, encouraging Ailsa to write Lyle, just to see how he was doing and how was his life. Jumping out of bed, she grabbed a pen and paper, ran to her desk, and resolved to write Lyle while the sweet memories were fresh in her mind. She wrote, reminding him of the wonderful time they had together. She told him how much she cared for him and knew they would always be friends. Aniel's powerful suggestion was to focus on the correspondence, guiding Ailsa to include in the letter that she wished he would respond just to keep each other informed about how their lives were going. I believe she really loves him. She does not know he is divorced and wants to renew their friendship. When Lyle showed up for work, Ailsa's letter was setting on his desk. As he walked to the desk, noticing the letter, he thought, "Who would be sending me a letter?" As he sat down, his heart jumped into his throat. It was from Scotland. There was only one person he knew lived there. Interestingly, you reported, he dreamed of her often after his divorce. You assumed it was his way of relieving his pain. This dream brought him some peace, remembering Ailsa's compassion and consoling him after his friend had killed himself. His heart was in his throat. He opened it, wondering why she was writing after all these years. His first fear was someone was informing she had died. The fleeting thought was present, remembering the death of Eva. As he cautiously opened the letter, slowly reading the first few lines, great joy swelled up in his heart. It was from Ailsa, and she was doing well. Ailsa's letter lifted his spirits, reminding him of all the fun they had together hanging in the village and eating meals together. This was one of two letters he received. The letters were labeled "letter #1" and "letter #2." (Readers, you must understand that in those years the internet did not exist. Letters were the best and inexpensive method for communicating to loved ones and friends.) Many people numbered their letters. This would ensure no misunderstanding would occur. Consider if no numbering was being used, letter (1) discusses someone falling and breaking an arm and letter (2) discussing the arm is healing. Now what would someone think if letter (2) was received first? Holy smokes, the broken arm was healing. WHAT HAPPENED? Landline phones were used, but telephone calls were expensive, especially international calls. Leuviah, I saw these letters brought you and him great joy. You reported he had not been so unburdened and happy for these long three years. He immediately responded, telling Ailsa how he enjoyed her letters and reminiscing about the time two friends had together. Lyle informed her he had been divorced for the past three years and how difficult his life had been; lonely, not being able to trust people. He expressed his desire to continue to communicate with her. Lyle asked her to include in the letter her daily activities as if they were sitting at the café enjoying a meal together. He said a silent prayer, thanking God for his good fortune. It was so pleasing to see him coming closer to the light, climbing out of his despair and darkness. Not to say all is well, but this may help him to move on from his terrible experience.

Diminish the demons.

Briathos

Leuviah, my loyal colleague,

You efforts have not been in vain. Lyle is attending services and praying as he did in the past. Although, I see he has been meditating. He is also attending Buddhist temples, meditating, and chanting to Buddha. I see he has also attended Temple and is reading the Torah. Confusion is in him as he works through this religious struggle. Driven by the black hole left from the divorce, he is searching for meaning and an emotional uplift in the form of letters from Ailsa. Remember, your responsibility is to encourage him to prayer. His free will is a danger to him. Do your best to keep him moving in our direction. I heard him say that he is questioning his belief in God. Lyle feels he has lost his soul. To him, his soul feels empty. There is something missing, but he cannot reconcile with what the missing component is; thus, meditating on Buddha and reading the Torah. This gives you a clearer picture on why he is searching different religions to find his way. The devi is back, encouraging him to attend the local Buddhist temple and pray to Buddha for strength and guidance in his life. I see Lyle is attending the local temple and chanting Buddhist mantras as he works through his religious turmoil. He is also attending Christian services and praying to God for guidance. I see his confusion and feelings of a void that cannot be filled. He wonders, "Can Buddha or God fill me with the spirit that will make me whole again? I feel as if something has torn my soul out so there is nothing there. I feel dead inside. Maybe there is nothing after death?" Stay close. He will need your guidance. The demons are busy at work, confusing him, telling him, "There is nothing after death. Why should you be concerned about being a godly person when in the end you are just dead?" They are pushing him to atheism. It is their hope he will die, denouncing God, so they can drag him kicking and screaming to hell. The soulless demons are salivating, just thinking about feasting on Lyle's soul. Our hope is he will resolve his search and fill the emptiness he feels with the Holy Spirit. On a positive note, I see letters are being sent and received daily between Ailsa and Lyle. I hope you are encouraging this. You reported speaking to Aniel (Ailsa's guardian angel), requesting he keep whispering sweet reminders to Ailsa to write. You say that Lyle is so uplifted by these letters, and he seems to be displaying a positive outlook. When I heard Ailsa was planning to visit him, I was hopeful both would see the love and happiness each could give one another. You know the demons will be scheming to corrupt this. Remind Aniel the team needs to be ever so vigilant. Of course, your reports can never go off without describing some type of incident involving Lyle. He was driving home from the city. Suddenly, a vehicle with three men in it drove next to him, pointing guns and screaming to pull over. Demons actually sneered at you, telling you that this time, they would have these humans KILL Lyle! You encouraged him not to stop or pull over. It could be disastrous. One of the men pointed his gun at the jeep and shot out the tire. The vehicle careened off the road to the right, sliding into a small ditch. He was able to stop without serious damage to the vehicle. The vehicle with the three men in it stopped ten yards in front of the Jeep. They jumped out and were running toward Lyle, screaming, "Get out of the car. Give us your money." The men wanted to carjack the vehicle, but because of the flat tire, it was impossible. They resolved to beat and rob him. Demons were yelling in the men's ears, enraging them further, "Kill him. KILL HIM!" As the men closed, one man yelled, "Let's kill him. He kept us from stealing the car." The criminals did not know that Lyle was licensed to carry a fire arm. As the men closed within twenty feet, Lyle jumped out of the jeep, pulled his pistol, and screamed, "Stop, don't make me shoot you." The men stopped for a heartbeat. Seeing the threat, they raised their weapons to fire. Because of the one-second delay, Lyle fired his weapon first, striking one men in the chest; groaning in pain, he fell to the ground. Another was hit directly in the face. Blood spewed out the back of his head as he fell backward dead. The third man began screaming, "I WILL KILL YOU!" He was firing wildly as he ran toward Lyle. Because of his training, Lyle remained steadfast, took aim at the assailant, and fired two rounds into the man's chest, killing him instantly. From a spiritual prospective, the carnage was disgusting. As the men dropped and died, at least ten demons were fighting over the three men's souls, tearing appendages so they had pieces for the nightly feast. The horrible screams coming from those men's souls were almost unbearable. The souls were just realizing this was only the beginning of enteral torment. Leuviah, I saw you standing in front of Lyle protecting him from the onslaught of bullets. He did not realize it was you who protected him. He thought it was blind luck that kept him from being hit. The local constabulary and emergency vehicles arrived. Lyle was taken to the police station to discuss the incident with detectives. After the interview, the detectives told Lyle that there would be an investigation into the shootings to further substantiate his version of the incident. Five days later, Lyle was called by the senior investigator, informing him that his investigation confirmed Lyle's story, and he was closing the case as self-defense. It was kind of you to say a prayer for the criminals and their families who had to suffer the pain of lost loved ones. We in the main office are concerned this incident may push Lyle back into the dark emotional hole he has been slowly climbing out of. Leuviah, impress upon Lyle that he had no other options but to shoot and kill the three men. This is one of the few times that God forgives the taking of a life. Evil requires to be crushed when there is no other alternative. God is disappointed that this had to happen, but when the enemy provokes events, the Father's children must respond.

Forever in your debt,
Briathos

Leuviah, God is with you.

I see this report covers multiple topics. There is much to unwind. You are having success with Lyle and his Christianity. Lyle has stopped going to the Buddhist temple or the Jewish temple's workshop. He is concentrating on Christianity. I heard him meditating using the meditation beads. Instead of chanting Buddhist mantras, he says small prayers. Lyle has been involved in church services, volunteering at the soup kitchens, and attending prayer meetings. He seems content with his life. Not to say he is isn't being challenged and sometimes falls back into that dark, angry place when he reflects on the evil his ex-wife had done. This turmoil was so deep in his soul; even after these three years, it can rear its ugly head, especially when the demons reminded him of the pain and anguish caused. He will sometimes daydream driving to where his ex-wife and friend are living and killing both of them slowly. It takes much work on your part to bring him back out of darkness and continue moving forward with Christ in his life. I see his correspondence with Ailsa has paid off. The first year, you reported each had traveled to the other's country for a visit. Their relationship grew exponentially. On his last visit to Scotland, he asked Ailsa to marry him. With great excitement, Ailsa accepted. There was a clear understanding that both loved and worship the Father and will be attending services together. One year later, Ailsa and Lyle were married. Two years after the wedding, they began taking in children to foster. These children had mothers and fathers who were having problems, from drug addiction, abuse, or convicted of a crime. They knew their love was strong. The desire was to provide a stable environment for these children to thrive in until the parents had gotten their lives together. As you pointed out, fostering children in difficult situations is challenging. They had to deal with angry parents. There was the drug dealer father with an addict mother incident. Ailsa and Lyle had their three-year-old daughter for care. The child was found hidden in a pile of newspapers during a drug raid. While fostering, the foster parents are responsible for taking the child to supervised visits with the parents. This allows for the children and parents to maintain a relationship while the system is helping to get them on track and regain custody of their child. During the third visit, the mother appeared to be high on drugs. She was screaming, "I want my child back now!" She grabbed the child and ran toward the exit. The father punched Lyle and knocked him down. The parents ran with the child out of the visiting center. Ailsa was screaming, "HELP, POLICE! They are taking the child." Suddenly, there were three policemen running down the hallway, asking Ailsa what had happened. Crying, she was barely able to tell them the parents had stolen the child and pointed toward the door they exited. Police ran into the parking lot, calling for patrol cars to get on scene. The parents jumped into a green van parked nearby and began to drive off. We guardian angels are so privileged to protect humans, especially young children. Ambrose (foster child's guardian angel) did such a wonderful job protecting and calming the child during this chaos. As we know, young, innocent children are able to see their guardian angels for the first few years of their lives. What a blessing. Seeing Ambrose and her beauty calmed the child. In a blink of an eye, two squad cars came roaring through the parking lot, and the first blocked the exit. The other pulled directly behind the van, eliminating any opportunity for escape. Not knowing whether the parents were armed, the police closed in on the van with guns drawn, yelling, "Come out with your hands raised." Seeing no escape, the parents slowly opened the doors and exited with their hands raised. The police closed in, handcuffed each person, and pulled the little girl out safely. Ailsa went running to the officer, the little girl literately jumped into her arms, crying, and saying, "I was so scared. The pretty lady in the van made me feel safe." Leuviah, tell Ambrosia the main office, including Archangel Michael, are proud of her work. Ailsa was able to calm the child. Lyle came walking out of the building, groggy from being hit, happy to see all was well. Leuviah, know that there will be an emotional toll placed on Ailsa and Lyle. There is an emotional strain placed on loving Humans who take in these children and love and care for them as if they were their own. Once the system has helped the parents, the child is given back under system supervision. The foster parents will never see the child again. There is an emotional toll feeling the loss of these children they learned to love. Because of this, demons are always attempting to cause chaos. They try to antagonize Ailsa and Lyle, coaxing them to be discontented with one another. With you and Aniel present, the demons' efforts can be thwarted. During the foster care interview process, Ailsa had requested no children under five years old for their home. Well, it never seems to work out as one would wish. God was testing them. The system contacted them, relating they had a three-week-old baby in the hospital who needed emergency placement. It was supposed to be a short-term placement, maybe for a month. Three years later, the child was still with them. Later that year, they received a call, telling them the system was returning the child to the parents. Ailsa and Lyle were stunned. They had raised the child for three years, and now she was being placed back with the parents. Lyle was angry, and he wanted to fight for the child's custody. Demons were pushing to do this, telling him, "You have raised her for her entire life. She is yours. Do not let them take her." With the help of Ailsa and her love, Lyle calmed and accepted the outcome. Lyle realized however devastating it was for him and Ailsa, he could not imagine how difficult it was for the child. She saw Lyle and Ailsa as her parents. She was Lyle's little buddy. They watched hockey together, cheering and having such fun. They had such a wonderful bond. Lyle had a difficult time with what was going to happen. He had taught her that when he said, "Mackenzie who is pop," she would throw her hands in the air, smile, and yell, "POP'S THE KING." I know you were doing all you could to remind Lyle they had gotten into foster care to be temporary guardians to the children. Words cannot describe Lyle's feelings; he was so sad. During the exchange, as dynamic as children can be, they seem to recognize the situation and bring calm to chaos. Lyle was holding the girl for their last hug. He was crying, holding her as tight as he could. During the hug, the little girl whispered to him, "it's ok, Daddy, I will be ok. I love you still." Heaven wept! During the three years taking care of the baby, the family had many children come through their house. They adopted two little girls and were raising them to be wonderful adults who loved their parents unconditionally. Lyle is now a deacon of the local church. Ailsa volunteers at the church helping needy families. They girls are growing with Christ. Leuviah, you and Aniel have done a great job keeping both Lyle and Ailsa in God's love. It is amazing how when God's children bend to his will and love and praise him, their lives seem to be calm and steady. That is not to say there will not be issues in the future. The enemy is always angling to cause chaos and draw souls to the dark side. You, Ambrose, and Aniel have given this family the tools to remain in God's light.

Be well, my sister.

Briathos

Leuviah

Sometimes I forget how short human lives are. Lyle and Ailsa are in their eightieth years, far beyond the twilight. I see that Ailsa met Aniel on her eighty-second birthday. Aniel was present at the end and escorted Ailsa to heaven to be with the Father. Although Lyle had been sad and lonely, he thanked God every day for the wonderful years he spent with Ailsa. Many humans search their entire lives trying to find that true soul mate. He often remembers back on the life they shared fondly recalling their initial meeting to reuniting years later. Then, he had the most beautiful union humans could expect. Leuviah, you have done well protecting and guiding Lyle through the eighty-plus years. You had many close calls. I expected many times you thought you were going to lose him to the enemy. You prevailed. God's love has always shown through you. The most touching moment, when reading your last report, was Lyle's passing. On the night before his eighty-fourth birthday, he lay in bed, so passionately remembering his love Aisla and their wonderful life. At 12:01, the first minute of his birthday, he passed in his sleep. I noticed you were lying next to him, waiting for the passing so he could be lifted up to heaven and be reunited with his love. As he passed, his soul rose, turned to his right, looked at you with a big smile, and said, "Hello, you must be the guardian angel who saved me so many times throughout my life. Thank you. I have had the most wonderful life a person could have." You said, "Welcome home, brother. I will now take you to the Father and reunite you with Ailsa." The light in his soul shined brightly with joy and happiness. I saw you both ascend to the gates. There stood Saint Peter, and as you approached him, you pointed to Lyle. Saint Peter, in an angelic voice, said, "Welcome, my brother. You have earned eternal life with the Father." The gates opened. As he walked through the most beautiful gates shining, he was in awe of the celestial light that appeared. Lyle knelt down. He was overwhelmed with the power and energy he felt. A powerful, calm, loving voice spoke and said, "Welcome home, my good and faithful servant." As the light diminished, Lyle saw Ailsa standing there with his mother, father, and other family members smiling with open arms. Ailsa said, "My love, I have been waiting for you to come." They shared an embrace, glowing with angelic happiness. He also greeted and hugged other relatives who had gone before him. Leuviah, you have exceeded God's expectations in your assignment. Lyle is here with the Father because of your guidance and love. Now one additional task must be accomplished. You will discuss with Lyle the journey he must embark upon to be cleansed of the sins he committed. You have been assigned to escort and guide Lyle through purgatory as he purges his sins committed on earth. This is his last quest that must be completed before eternal access to heaven is given; a small price to pay for eternal life and happiness. Amen.

God be with you always,
Briathos

Dear Reader—As I see you have completed following Leuviah's trials while protecting Lyle in his challenging life. Guardian angels are the unsung heroes of the Father, silently coaxing their assignment to maintain God's spirituality throughout their lives. The enemy is strong (on earth) because the Father has given him free reign over it and the inhabitants. His efforts are to corrupt the humans and take as many to hell for feasting as can possibly be obtained. As you should have noticed throughout Lyle's life, the demons (tools of Satan) were ever present, pressing him to join the blackness and anguish of hell. This is not the only human needing guidance, and as you have seen, many guardian angels worked in concert to save Lyle and other souls around him. You can see how devious the enemy is and experienced the torment given to those souls who were consumed by the darkness when their lives expired. Anguish and pain are the enemy's tools of his trade. Keep this in mind as you walk through your life. The enemy is diligent, and my guardian angels are well prepared to fight the battle for each and every soul on earth. There is eternal life, and it can be yours by following the path set out by the Father and guided by your guardian angel. Remember those events in your life where you were in danger, and some unknown urge, or thought came to you, saying, "Jump," or "Cry out" or "Duck" that kept you from being injured. Maybe you were in an automobile accident, and the medical experts expressed, "You should not be alive." Think of your guardian angel. They are always there. Just listen; a whisper, a nudge, maybe a passing thought, causing you to stop and think. They are there. Be open to them. It may save your life. Join Leuviah as she navigates Lyle through his quest in purgatory repenting.

Glossary

Archangel Michael
Know as the "Angel Captain" or "Chief Prince." Lead Angel, responsible for keeping all Angels on task as order by God.
Briathos (Angel that thwarts demons)
Reports to Michael. Trains and monitors all Guardian Angels. Maintains communications between himself and Guardian Angels, as they work protecting their assigned Humans. Briathos provides guidance and encouragement to assigned Guardian Angels.
Leuviah (Symbolizes letting go)
Helps those who call upon her to combat Human malice. Protector of Lyle as he moves through his life.
Rizoel (Angel with power to thwarts demons)
His name means "secret God." Assigned to Lyle's father as protector and guide.

Karael (Angel has the power to thwart demons)
Assigned to Lyle's mother as protector and guide.
Engels (Angel prince of dreams)
Failed to protect his Charge, who committed suicide.
Jeliel (Name means God's helper)
Helps distinguish between illusion and authenticity. Assisted Leuviah, to guide and save sailors trapped on a ship because of a mine explosion.

Sitael (Angel of repentance)
Assisted Leuvian, to guide and save sailors trapped on a ship because of a mine explosion.
Cahetel (Angel of benevolance)
Guardian of John. She failed to protect him. Her Charge committed suicide, jumping overboard from a ship.
Hahaiah (The hope of all creatures on earth)
Guides Humans when preparing for rites and ceremonies. Assigned to Lyle's wife, whom committed adultry.

Seheiah (God who heals the sick)
Linked tolongevity and health for a happy life. Assigned to Lyle's oldest daughter.
Aniel (Angel of virtues)
Spirit guide of will and determination. Encourages people to act with stdrength. Protector and guardian for Ailsa.
Poyel (Angel of support and fortune)
Brings joy and humor into Human's daily life. Responsible for children and their innocence.
Azrael (Angel of Death)
Responsible for ensuring and escorting souls to Heaven or Hell.
Mebahiah (Eternal Angel, symbolizes inspiration)
Spreads ideas relating to spirituality. Provides comfort and care to Lyle's history teacher.
Ambrose (Brings clarity to mental harmony)

CPSIA information can be obtained
at www.ICGtesting.com
Printed in the USA
BVHW042356141022
649426BV00001B/74